WESTERN

W9-BXR-673

Large Print Sve
Svee, Gary D., 1943—
Sanctuary

SANCTUARY

Also by Gary D. Svee
in Thorndike Large Print

Incident at Pishkin Creek

SANCTUARY

Gary D. Svee

Thorndike Press • Thorndike, Maine

Library of Congress Cataloging in Publication Data:

Svee, Gary D., 1943-
    Sanctuary / Gary D. Svee.
        p. cm.
    ISBN 1-56054-143-1 (alk. paper : lg. print)
    1. Large type books. I. Title.
[PS3569.V37S25   1991]   91-10211
813'.54—dc20   CIP

All the characters and events protrayed in this work are
fictitious.

Thorndike Press Large Print edition published in 1991
by arrangement with McIntosh & Otis, Inc.

Cover design by James B. Murray.

The tree indicium is a trademark of Thorndike Press.

This book is printed on acid-free, high opacity paper.

I dedicate this book to my mother, Beatrice Evelyn Svee, who spoke no English as a young child and has spoken only kindness since.

One

The train was late, but Judd Medicine Elk didn't know that, nor did he care. He had been pulled from his blankets by the cold and the ache in his belly and habit. That was all he needed to know. So he waited, dancing from one foot to the other for warmth and to ease the hunger that coursed from his belly to his brain.

Perhaps he would be lucky today. Strangers on the train might give him a nickel or a dime for carrying their luggage from the depot to a waiting buggy or to Sanctuary's only hotel.

Perhaps, too, the agent would open the door of a freight car and he could steal something of value, something he could trade for food for himself and his grandmother.

The cold hung on the land like a curse, and Judd tried to chase it away with the magic of his dance. The sole of one shoe — several sizes too big for his twelve-year-old foot — was peeled back to the heel, and it slapped first the platform and then his foot, beating a crude cadence.

Slap, slap, flop. Slap, slap, flop.

The rhythm stirred Judd, and his dance changed tone and tempo, his feet, nerves, muscles, sinews hearing the shuffling steps of moccasined feet on ancient plains. No longer did the men of the Cree tie their bleeding flesh to a pole or a buffalo skull with skewers and thongs to sacrifice their pain to their god in the Thirst Dance. Now they danced only when they could find a bottle of whiskey, but still they danced in great pain.

Slap, slap, flop. Slap, slap, flop.

Judd danced now to thank the manitou for the threadbare clothing that kept him warm except when the cruel north wind howled through Sanctuary. He thanked the Cree god for the food he hoped to have today.

His grandmother had told him about the manitou and the Christian God. She had become a Christian when the white man's God had driven the manitou from the plains. She knew the Cree god had gone away, because he would not have allowed his people to suffer so.

But the Christ God seemed uninterested in old Cree women, and now she believed in nothing. Judd prayed to the manitou because he believed himself to be invisible to the white man's God. Judd believed he was

8

invisible to all white men.

Light flooded the railroad station, and Judd froze. If the agent saw the boy waiting on the platform, he would chase him away.

The agent stepped out on the platform, and Judd stopped breathing so that the plume that followed his breath into the cold air would not give him away.

But the agent was looking down the track. He pulled a gold pocket watch from his vest and read it for the second time in five minutes. The watch slipped back into the agent's pocket, and his eyes flicked across the platform, hesitating for no more than a blink on Judd. He shook his head and walked back into the station, shivering.

Judd's breath hissed into the air through clenched teeth. Safe! He was still invisible. Sometimes dancing made him visible.

The train came sharp, black, and shiny, fleeing a cloud of white steam and coal smoke. It howled then, lonesome as a coyote, and sparks flew from the wheels as the engineer set the brakes.

Judd was fascinated by this great beast. He dreamed sometimes of stepping aboard one of the cars and riding it to someplace where he had never been, someplace different from where he was.

But that was only a dream, and his hunger

was a gnawing reality. He shook away the pain in his gut and focused his attention on the train, stepping closer to the engine, closer to the heat and the steam.

The redolence of burning coal sifted over the boy, and Judd breathed deeply. Sometimes coal spilled along the track and he carried it to his grandmother's one-room shanty where it burned the barrel stove dull red on cold winter days. Coal was warmth and rabbit stew simmering in a cast-off, cast-iron pot.

Judd stiffened. A black porter stepped down from a Pullman and put the step in place for detraining passengers. He peered for a moment at the skinny kid in cast-off, ragtag clothes and long, stringy hair — Montana Indians were as much a mystery to him as black men were to Judd. The glance pacified the porter's curiosity, and he went back to his work.

A drummer followed the porter from the train. He was scowling, and Judd stepped deeper into the steam. Drummers were good — sometimes. One had given him a quarter for carrying only two bags to the hotel. But sometimes with drummers, it was better to be invisible.

This drummer sauntered into the station, slamming the door behind him. He reappeared a moment later and grabbed his bags, glaring at Judd as he stalked back into the building.

Judd was left alone on the platform. He watched the train take on water so alkaline it had to be seasoned with chemicals to make it potable for the steam engine. The engine drank in one long steady pull from the tank perched on wooden legs above the track. Then it stood like a huge, contented animal, breathing steam and hissing.

The boy jumped just a little as the locomotive whistled its warning. Then a shudder rattled the train, traveling from car to car down the track until it reached the caboose, where the conductor leaned out to watch the cars and the track ahead. The locomotive blew a huge cloud of steam and edged away, wheels slipping at first and then taking hold. Judd stepped back to watch, listening as the *clickety-clack* of steel striking steel built to a crescendo.

The caboose emerged from the cloud and passed Judd, pulling some of the steam and Judd's thoughts after it. He watched it until it disappeared around the bend where the track ran between the bluff and the Milk.

As Judd turned for the stairs, he saw a shape emerging from the steam. Tall, he was, and slim in a dark suit and a clerical collar. A preacher had come to town. At

11

first Judd thought the man might have been riding the rods, hanging beneath a car for a wild trip across the Montana prairie.

But even as the thought crossed his mind, he discarded it.

No railroad bull had ever pulled this man from a train. There was a sense of certainty about him, but gentleness, too.

The preacher looked at Judd and smiled. The smile warmed the boy, taking the sting from the cold spring morning. But Judd poised to run, wary as that coyote last winter. The coyote, torn between hunger and fear that the dead rabbit in Judd's snare was bait for a trap, had worn a circle in the snow. When Judd came that morning to check the snare, the animal plunged away.

Was the preacher's smile a promise or a trap?

The preacher's hair hung just over his collar, his face was thin, ascetic, and topped by a high forehead too deeply tanned for this time of year. The stranger's eyes were brown and warm, yet piercing. Judd felt drawn to the man — and afraid.

"Follow me," the preacher said, and Judd picked up the stranger's valise, light as a thought on a warm spring day, and followed him down the steps and into the street.

Judd didn't know if the stranger had been

in Sanctuary before, or if he just had a sense for small Montana towns, where hotels would be and what they would look like. But he walked directly to the hotel, Judd following behind on the boardwalk.

Slap, slap, flop. Slap, slap, flop.

Judd usually avoided the town's main street. He was vulnerable there, glaring eyes shucking him of his invisibility as one shucks the husk from an ear of corn. Open to the townsfolk's eyes, he was open to their contempt. But now he was carrying the preacher's valise. Surely they would not object to that.

The preacher stopped at the hotel's front door and dropped a coin into Judd's hand. A quarter! Judd held the coin tightly, not trusting the pockets in his patched and repatched pants to hold the treasure. At the slaughterhouse, he could buy two livers and perhaps a beef heart for a quarter unless Jasper was there; then the price would be high — too high. Judd shuddered.

Today, he and his grandmother would eat, and he thanked the manitou for that great blessing.

The preacher was staring at him, a gentle smile on his face, and Judd was torn between running back to the safety of his shack and staying in the warmth of that smile.

"Name's Mordecai," the preacher said,

holding out his hand. Judd took it tentatively, never having shaken hands before.

"Your name?"

"Judd." The boy spoke as though in apology.

"That isn't all of it, is it?"

Judd's eyes narrowed. "Medicine Elk," he whispered.

"You stick close, Judd. I'm likely to have need of you before I get shut of this."

Judd's eyes darted up the street and down. Not many people out yet. Sunday morning like this most folks were in church listening to the Reverend Eli Timpkins scare the hell out of them. But after services, the boardwalks would fill with bonnets and tight collars and righteousness, and the people of Sanctuary would try to kill Judd with their eyes.

He didn't want to stay, but he didn't want to leave either — like that dog last winter.

Judd's mind drifted back to early December. A border collie had streaked away from the step as Judd pushed open the door of the shack, carving a wide, deep arc in the new-fallen snow.

The dog, for reasons unfathomable to Judd, had bedded on an old burlap sack on the step. He streaked away as Judd opened the door, snow spraying from each of his leaps.

The slaughterhouse hadn't operated for

14

nearly a week. Soup gleaned from deer bones and grain scraped from the ground near the railroad tracks had carried them for several days, but now even that was gone. Certainly no scraps were lying about to attract the animal.

Judd had spent the past two days huddled beside a stove, feeble against the cold that had blown in from the Arctic and was hanging like a specter over the land. And all that time he watched his grandmother, her face gaunt with hunger, pale, as though life were draining from her, belly first.

Judd didn't know if the snowstorm had followed the dog or the dog had followed the storm, but they both arrived the same night, both haunting the shack like hunger.

Each morning the dog would be curled at the corner of the step, only to bolt away when Judd, shaking with cold, opened the door and made his way to the woodpile.

And as Judd loaded his arms with branches cast off by cottonwoods on the river bottom, the dog would sit and watch fifty feet away as though that distance made him invisible. Sometimes Judd talked to the animal about how cold it was and what his grandmother had said and how he wished he had food to share with the dog.

The dog, belly pulled tight to backbone,

played in Judd's thoughts during the day and in his dreams at night. Judd knew what it was to be hungry and invisible, and he wanted to feed the dog almost as much as he wanted to feed his grandmother.

Then, when Judd thought he could no longer tolerate the cold and the hunger and the cries of younger children howling nearby like the wind around the shacks, the sky cleared to a day so cold that century-old cottonwoods split with the crack of cannon fire on the river bottom.

The boy felt his grandmother's eyes on him as he dressed, and he sensed the weight of her need. He strapped on his makeshift snowshoes and shuffled toward the Milk through snow squeaking its protest of the cold. The dog followed for a while, whining but coming no closer than fifty feet, and Judd talked to the animal about the cold that burned his face red and then white and how he hoped rabbits had found his snares because *the people* were so hungry.

But the dog followed only a little way before the whining stopped, and Judd turned to watch the animal limp back toward the shack, followed the trail they had carved in the deep snow. The boy pushed on.

The river bottom was crisscrossed with rabbit tracks, but the snares were empty, buried under three feet of snow. He reset the simple devices with fingers stiff and clumsy as sticks. Then he trudged back to the shack, weak with hunger and despair.

As he leaned against the shack to shake the snow from his snowshoes, Benjamin Two Teeth stepped out, carrying fresh, bloody meat. He avoided Judd's eyes and waded through the snow to his own shack, where the children had been crying for two days.

Inside, Judd was greeted with the smell of boiling meat. Tough the meat was, and stringy, but to Judd it was delicious.

And after he and his grandmother had eaten and Judd had rubbed his fingers clean on his shirt, he asked his grandmother where she had gotten the meat.

"It is a gift of the manitou," she said in Cree.

It wasn't until later, when the snow began to melt, that Judd found the dog's skull behind the cabin. He knew then why the dog had haunted the cabin.

But Judd didn't tell the preacher about the dog. He nodded and slipped back into the narrow space between the hotel and the leather shop, breathing deeply to catch the scent of new saddles and harness and shoes.

He ducked into the alley at the back of

the building and followed the preacher, catching glimpses of him in the flashes of dark and light between buildings. The preacher walked along the boardwalk, heels clattering against wood, nodding to curious passersby, and Judd followed in the alley, furtive and silent, desperately willing himself invisible.

The preacher stepped into the Silver Dollar Cafe, and Judd waited in the alley, his belly tied in a knot. The smell of frying onions and hot grease reminded him of how hungry he was. A spasm racked him, and he wrapped his arms around his gut, doubling over with pain. His eyes filled with tears for a moment, blurring everything around him, and he was ashamed of himself.

When the pain passed and Judd had pushed himself erect, the preacher was standing beside him.

"Bought a couple of steaks, these eggs, and some potatoes for you," the preacher said. "Take them home and have some breakfast. I'll see you later."

Judd shook his head.

"Don't you have somebody at home, boy, who would enjoy this?"

"How did you know I was here?"

"Saw you. Take the food, Judd. I wouldn't feel right eating with you standing out here hungry. So if you don't take this, I'll go hungry and you'll go hungry and your grand-mother will go hungry."

"I have money," Judd said, opening his hand to reveal the quarter.

"You have money *and* food," the preacher corrected.

Judd stared into the preacher's eyes, trying to read what was hidden beyond. Then, he took the food and fled, running for the shack as a ground squirrel runs for his hole when the shadow of a hawk floats by. And each step Judd took, each breath he drew, the question nagged at him. How did the preacher know about his grandmother?

Mordecai shoved back from the table, tip-ping his chair on its back legs. Breakfast had been good — the best he'd had in years — and he lingered at the table, sipping his third cup of coffee and picking at his teeth with a splinter.

Mordecai stretched and stood, then stepped around tables to the hall that tied the Silver Dollar Cafe with the Silver Dollar Saloon.

The hall was dark, and Mordecai smelled the saloon before he saw it — sour beer, stale cigar smoke, the smell of unwashed bodies. Saloons were pretty much the same wherever they were.

Sunday morning had driven most of the

crowd home to sleep off Saturday night, but for some the Silver Dollar was home. They were gathered now in familial knots of two and three, nursing from shared bottles.

All eyes focused on the preacher's collar as he stepped through the door, and the regulars huddled closer together. Damn shame, they muttered, when even the sanctity of the Silver Dollar was invaded by preachers.

Mordecai settled at one end of a mahogany bar so dark and richly carved it gave the room a gothic air. That impression was enhanced by the rows of stuffed heads that lined the walls — great, dead animals surveying the dimly lit scene with glass eyes.

"What'll you have?"

The bartender was short and wiry, the white apron he wore an accent point painted into a melancholic picture too somber to be real. While he waited for Mordecai's order, he polished glasses with a clean, white towel, snapping it as he finished each glass.

"Three fingers of red eye."

The bartender cocked his head, staring at Mordecai. "Got some coffee — good and stout."

"Bar whiskey."

The bartender nodded. "Name's Ben," he said, offering his hand. ". . . Johnson."

"Mordecai," the preacher replied, taking

20

Johnson's hand.

Whispers followed the preacher's first sip of the whiskey. He was all right, they said. Can't fault a man of the cloth who owns up to having a taste for whiskey. Preachers need a drink once in a while just like everyone else. Only thing is that some of them won't admit it.

The preacher settled back, for a moment forgotten. He watched as the back door opened and a grizzled creature in an ancient, tattered suit slouched through. He wore a white beard, the product not of intent but of neglect.

Johnson set an empty glass on the bar. The old man stiffened then, studying the glass as a starving wolf studies a lone sheep.

He nodded, his lips moving in a conversation only he could hear, and shuffled to a closet. He reached inside for a push broom and a box of oiled sawdust, then stopped, staring at the bar until Johnson poured the glass full of whiskey. The old man nodded again and resumed his conversation with himself. He took a scoop of oiled sawdust and shuffled determinedly toward the front door, spraying sawdust from his shaking hand. He paused after each trip to the barrel, to look at the glass of whiskey and to wet his lips.

"Name's Doc," Johnson said to Mordecai,

propping his elbows on the bar. "Old Army doctor, rode with Colonel Miles. Told me one time that he was up in the Bear Paws when Chief Joseph turned himself in."

Mordecai nodded. "How long's he been doing that?"

"Swamping? He's been here longer than I have. I 'spect he'll be here long after I've gone . . . if his liver holds out. Man who owned the Silver Dollar before me gave him a place out back. Didn't see any reason to take it away from him."

The old man worked steadily, the *swish, swish, thump* of the broom broken only by the scrape of wood on wood as he moved tables and chairs. When he finished, he circled the room, dumping cigar and cigarette butts into a spittoon still awash from the night before. Then he carried the other spittoons out back, presumably to empty and wash them.

"Does a good job," Johnson said, returning from a trip to one of the tables. "At least so long as that whiskey glass sits on the bar. Give him a drink first, and he's done for the day."

The old man returned, put the spittoons in their receptacles at the bar and on the floor by the tables, then shuffled toward the bar, wiping his reddened hands on his pant legs. He shuddered to a stop and stared at the glass of whiskey. The quiet talk stopped, and everyone turned to watch the morning routine.

Doc ran his tongue around his lips and reached for the drink, hand shaking violently. He tried to pick up the glass, but some whiskey spilled on the bar and the old man set the glass down so hard more sloshed out.

Doc leaned over and pressed his lips down on the bar next to the glass, but before he licked up the whiskey, he felt the eyes on his neck. He stood then, pulling himself to attention like the old soldier he was.

"Here, Doc," Johnson said. The old man looked up as the bartender launched a wadded bar towel at him. He nodded, and draped the towel around his neck, holding the short end with his left hand. Grasping the long end of the towel with his right hand stopped the shaking, and he was able to pick up the glass. He pulled the towel slowly around his neck, the tension keeping his hand steady until the glass was at his lips.

He took a deep sip, and for a moment it appeared that the old man's knees would buckle. He waited until the alcohol seeped into his system and then dropped the towel, his hands steady. He took another sip.

"Sweet Mary," one of the men whispered reverently. "There is a man who loves good whiskey."

The preacher set his glass down on the bar. "Have any port?" he asked Johnson.

Johnson nodded.

"And some glasses — eight."

Johnson walked down the bar to collect the order, and Mordecai slipped off the bar stool.

"I want to buy a drink for the house!" the preacher announced, and all eyes turned to him. "Over here by the window."

Raised eyebrows and shrugs circled the tables, but the Silver Dollar regulars clumped across the hard oak floor and settled into the two tables by the door. Maybe they would get two shows this morning.

"First," the preacher said. "We'll bow our heads."

Some of the men were digging I-told-you-so elbows into their neighbors' ribs. But they all bowed their heads, some necks creaking like rusty pump handles with the effort.

"Our Father who art in heaven . . ."

Most of the men mumbled along, memories of their youth tumbling into their minds as the prayer continued. And some were silent, afraid of being branded as religious by their friends.

Doc was hanging at the back of the group, and the preacher said, "Come on, Doc, have a glass of wine with us."

But Doc shook his head. "That wine's too bitter for me."

The preacher walked around the two tables, passing out crackers he had taken from the bar.

" 'Take and eat: This is my Body, which is given for you. Do this in remembrance of me.' "

And then he passed out glasses of wine.

" 'This is the Blood of the new Covenant, which is shed for you and for many for the forgiveness of sins. Whenever you drink it do this for the remembrance of me.' "

The preacher was almost at the end of the line when a loud chorus of mismatched voices accompanied by a bass drum broke in on the simple ceremony. "Onward Christian Soldiers" filled the bar with sanctimony.

"Guess it's our turn," one of the regulars said, and the others guessed he was right. The preacher caught his eye, and the man explained.

"Well, the Reverend Eli gets the good folk of Sanctuary up to church on Sunday and gets them all riled up about us sinners. Then he picks the sinner of the week, and the Christian soldiers march onward. Sometimes they roost down here, sometimes over at the — uh, cribs; sometimes at one sinner's house or another.

"The Reverend'll start yelling at us pretty quick, and after he's told everybody what he thinks of us, they'll all march back to the church feeling real good about themselves. I guess you might say that us sinners do those folks a real service." Nods followed that observation.

"Let's celebrate that," the preacher said, moving down the line, continuing to pass out the glasses of wine.

Just as Mordecai was serving the last man, the door to the Silver Dollar opened and the Reverend Eli Timpkins poked into the bar. The Reverend was tall, skinny, and hard, the heat of his passions having burned away all softness long ago. His righteousness raged and blazed within him, and sweat ran down his face as though to cool the furnace within. His brows were bushy and pulled down tight over eyes burning with righteousness. Those eyes blazed through the room before settling on Mordecai.

"Blasphemy!" The word spewed from the Reverend like the rumble and hiss of a geyser erupting from the bowels of the earth. "It was the Lord who led me here today to witness this blasphemer" — his finger settled like the barrel of a pistol on Mordecai's nose — "who offers the Lord's holy sacrament to these miserable sinners in this place of depravity."

26

Mordecai, his hand resting on the last man's shoulder, continued the litany, ". . . This is my blood of the new Covenant which is shed for you and for many for the forgiveness of sins. Whenever you drink it, do this for the remembrance of me."

Some of the men began rising from the table.

"See you next week," Mordecai said, "and since the good gentleman has raised the question, I'll talk about blasphemy, although I lack the expertise the Reverend apparently has."

Laughter rippled around the tables, peppered with "We'll be heres," and the Reverend Eli's face twisted with rage.

"Those who mock the Lord shall be cast down into hell to suffer damnation and eternal fire!" The words hissed from the Reverend's mouth as though his soul were already sizzling.

"And those who *make* a mockery of the Lord will have their toes warmed at that same fire," Mordecai said.

Another round of hoots echoed through the bar, and the Reverend shook with rage. He stalked from the bar, legs shaking, but before he stepped through the door, he turned, his eyes opaque and aimed at Mordecai's heart.

"I will see you in hell!"

"Could be you'll be waiting for me."

Mordecai followed the Reverend outside. The town's good folk were gathered there wrapped in their righteousness and their Sunday go-to-meeting best.

"Before you come marching down Main Street in search of other sinners to humiliate," Mordecai said, "might be you'll look for the logs in your own eyes."

Some of the men and women on the edge of the crowd shifted, suddenly fascinated by the boardwalk under their feet. The Reverend raised his fist for the drummer, and the beat began, but it was not as measured as it had been when the group arrived, and there were more stragglers than marchers making their way back to the white frame church at the far end of Main Street.

The saloon regulars crowded around the door to watch the final scene in the show that morning — all except for one.

Doc stood rooted near the stool where the preacher had been sitting, his foot covering the gold double eagle he'd spotted on the floor. He wanted to move, to reach down and pick up the coin, but he was afraid that if he did, someone would spot him and claim it.

So Doc stumbled, lurched into the bar, and fell to the floor, his hand scrabbling for the coin. Nobody would think anything odd about an old drunk falling down.

Two

"Where you headed, Doc?"

Doc stopped mid-shuffle, pinioned to the floor. He had hoped to escape the saloon unseen, but he knew that wasn't likely. He was as much a fixture of the place as the bottles lined up on the back bar and his absence just as noticeable.

"Out back," he croaked, his voice over-burdened with guilt and excitement.

"Already?" Johnson asked in mock amazement. "Boys, you are seeing the eighth wonder of the world. The man with the magic bladder only lasted 'til ten-thirty."

Hoots followed the old man into the alley. He wished he could pick up his feet, but he didn't have the energy or the balance, so it was better to keep both feet on the ground. His shuffling annoyed him, especially now when he needed to get away from the preacher, away from the preacher's eyes.

For the first time in years, there was something the old man needed to do away from the saloon. That was exciting, but frightening too. The Silver Dollar and alcohol were blankets he had pulled over himself after . . . no, he didn't want to think about that.

Best that he keep moving now, get someplace where he could get his mind working before the preacher noticed he was missing the twenty-dollar gold piece.

Twenty dollars! It was his ticket out of Sanctuary, a ticket back to the respectable life he had before that day in the Bear Paws . . . how many years ago? Doc shook his head. He wasn't even sure what year this was. The only thing he was sure about was the letter he always kept in his coat pocket, right there.

The old man's hands, shaking with dread, probed the pocket. Empty! The damn thing was empty! His eyes rolled, and he was shaking all over. No way out now. He'd be here in Sanctuary forever. His hands roved his tattered coat. He was frantic. How could he have lost the only hope he had? And then he heard the rustle of paper. Of course, he had changed pockets because the lining was torn, and he was afraid the letter would fall through and be swept away in one wind or another.

Doc almost swooned with relief.

He was back on track, now. He had the money and the letter. He sat on the step behind the clothing store. No one would bother him there, and he could think about what he needed to do.

He spent the evening fighting his need to go back to the saloon, willing his mind to function. Exhausted with the effort, he fell asleep, wedged in the corner of the door.

The cold and the ache in his neck awakened him before dawn. He pulled himself into a ball, hands squeezed tightly together. The old man was fighting for his life.

And as the sun sent shards of light over the Montana prairie, Surgeon Raleigh J. Benjamin sat rigid with pain on the alley step of the haberdashery, plotting his escape from Sanctuary as an innocent man might plot his escape from prison.

Clothes, of course, he would need a new suit. He looked at the suit he was wearing, seeing it for the first time in years, and he was shocked at its shabbiness.

Of course! That was the reason he had come to the haberdashery. Now he remembered. He sat on the step, wringing his hands. He had to make his mind work, shed himself of the fog he had thrown over himself years ago. He needed new clothing. That was the reason he hadn't been able to go home. That was the reason he had come to the store.

But he couldn't buy clothes now, not the way he was. First he had to get cleaned up. Doc ran his hand over a wispy beard. He'd need a shave, too.

So he had to get himself fit, then buy a suit of clothes and a ticket. No, he had a ticket.

He pulled the letter from his pocket, and began reading:

Dear Raleigh:

I hope this letter finds you in good health. I have bad news. My dear Emma has passed beyond. Dr. Smythe treated her to the end, but she finally turned her back on the pain and tribulations of this life, sighed, and stepped into her Maker's arms. She died as she had lived — in great beauty.

She remained fond of you, as, of course, I have, and one of the regrets of her life was your separation from the family after she and I married.

Neither of us could understand your rather reckless plunge into the army, but that was a matter of your own conscience, and we had no intention of shutting you out of our lives as you seem to have shut us out of yours.

Now I rattle about in the old family home, and it fairly echoes of Emma. I have taken of late to thinking of our youth together in this rambling estate and long to see you and make amends for whatever I might have done to alienate you. You, of course, are entitled to your share of the income from the various interests in which father invested. I might add that you have accumulated a considerable sum over the years.

I would think that time has salved the sting of whatever it was that drove you to the Montana wilderness, and I do not want to pass, as Emma did, without resolving our differences, whatever they might be. I didn't realize the depth of Emma's concern about your estrangement until I heard her calling your name from her sleep just a few days before she died.

Please return home, if only for a short visit. I would think you have fulfilled your obligation to humanity by your service these many years. I have enclosed a voucher for tickets to encourage your quick return. I remain

Your brother,
Marcus Scott Benjamin

Doc had received the letter the fall before; it was wrinkled and pocked with the tears he had shed on it. And after the tears, he had taken the voucher to the train depot to trade it for cash. But the agent explained that the voucher was good only for tickets. He had almost thrown it away then. He had no wish to see his brother again, not after Emma . . .

Raleigh didn't compete with his brother for Emma. He hadn't asked her that gentle spring to attend a ball or go riding or take a walk. But each time he saw her, his eyes sparkled like fool's gold on a creek bottom. He watched her with an intentness that frightened her sometimes, and his face flushed red whenever she was near.

Raleigh knew that Emma had cared for him, too. He knew that to a certainty until that night when Marcus had come to him, pacing, bobbing from one chair to the next. Emma had accepted his proposal.

Doc had drunk himself blind that night for the first time in his life. Drinking had made all the other times easier, especially after the Bear Paws.

He still felt the pain — not as sharp as his aching need for a glass of whiskey — but a dull pang that drilled into his consciousness whenever he went to bed sober enough for his mind to function.

That ache had driven him away from Atlanta, and he wouldn't be considering returning home now but for that day last winter when another pain in his abdomen had pulled him awake. That pain was easier to diagnose. His liver was enlarged and hard. Cirrhosis. The old man had seen enough men die of that disease to know that the end shouldn't be faced alone.

He had tried to stop drinking then, but couldn't.

But he could stop now. He had made it through the night without a drink, and he had money enough to get clothes and get cleaned up.

He could go home now and live the life of a gentleman. He imagined the servants at his beck and call. A few days a week at cards with friends from his youth. How he would like to see them.

And he should teach, share his experience with young doctors who would live their lives out without seeing the number and kinds of traumatic injuries he had. He guessed that he could give them a pointer or two about the care of their patients.

That thought warmed him. Doctor Raleigh J. Benjamin dropping by the hospital to lend his expertise. He tried to sit a little straighter, as befitted a man of his newfound stature, but he suddenly had a nagging need for a drink.

No! Nothing to drink! There was too much to do. First thing, he'd stop at the Barber

Pole and get a shave and a haircut. Nothing like that to get a man feeling good.

Charley the barber looked up as the bell tinkled above the door.

"Hi, Doc," he said, not bothering to climb out of his chair. Charley was a cowboy who retired when a bronc broke his hip into jagged, painful pieces. He could barely walk now, let alone ride a horse, but he could live with that, and every time a blizzard roared through Sanctuary he thanked that bronc for turning his life around. He didn't cut hair fancy, but a man got his money's worth, and Charley knew how to keep his opinions to himself.

"Little short on change, today," Charley said, turning his pockets inside out. "You know I'd help if I could."

Doc stood next to the door shaking his head violently. Doctor Raleigh J. Benjamin was no beggar . . . at least not today.

"Don't want charity," the old man said. "Want a haircut."

Charley tipped his head and looked Doc over, head to toe.

"Don't mean to offend, Doc, but I won't cut your hair 'less you take a bath. Got my other customers to think of."

Doc's eyebrows rose to make room for

the incredulity that spread across his face. That was no way to talk to Doctor Raleigh J. Benjamin, soon-to-be lecturer in the great medical centers of Atlanta, Georgia.

Charley watched the old man's face unravel. "Tell you what. I'll throw in the bath for free. Water's hot. You can go out back and soak that — soak those years right off you."

"I have money to pay," Doc said, holding the double eagle out for Charley to see.

"Told you, Doc, the bath's free, but you can pay me for the haircut. Couldn't change that gold piece for you, though."

Doc's mind was racing. "Charley, might be that while I get ready for the bath, you could change this for me at the haberdashery.

"And Charley, there's a suit there in the window. I remember seeing it now. Gray wool for four dollars and ninety-five cents. It'd fit me, I know it would. I measured my reflection in the window. I remember that now.

"Charley, if you could, maybe you'd bring me that suit and take out for the haircut . . . and take something for your trouble, too."

The old man's eyes were shining, and he looked at the barber as though the old cowboy were an angel about to perform a miracle.

"Reckon I could, Doc," Charley said so softly he could barely hear himself. "Reckon I could do that much for you."

37

"A shirt too," Doc called after him. "And a tie."

Doc walked out of the barbershop a new man. He had soaked off years of despair, along with layers of dirt. There was even a trace of a spring in his step as he walked toward the Silver Dollar bathed, clean-shaven, dressed in a new suit, and with the jingle of real money in his pocket.

He nodded at passersby on the street, pleased that they didn't recognize him as Silver Dollar Doc.

When he reached the saloon, he paused on the boardwalk, steadying himself against the hitching rail out front. This would be the hardest part, saying goodbye to Johnson and some of the others, but it had to be done, and quickly. Then he would go out back to the shack for a night's sleep, and on the train tomorrow morning.

He opened the door and stepped in. Johnson was sitting behind the bar, reading the weekly newspaper. Reading was a skill only recently acquired. Miss Dickens, the schoolmarm, had night classes for some of the adults in town, and he had been one of her star pupils. Still he read slowly, lips moving across the words. It took him about a week to finish the weekly paper.

Johnson looked up, settled back into the

paper, and then jerked his attention back to Doc.

"Doc?"

"It is I," Doc replied, sweeping his arms out in a theatrical greeting. But the movement was too much for his still shaky balance, and he grabbed the edge of a table to steady himself.

"I'll be damned," Johnson said. "Boys, let me present Doc, swamper of the Silver Dollar Saloon."

Doc bowed again, but less extravagantly than before.

Silence followed, and then babble. "Been coming in here for years — I didn't even know he could talk." "Kind of a distinguished old gent once he gets cleaned up." "Who died?"

"Going home," Doc croaked. "Going back to Atlanta to live out the rest of my years with my brother. I just wanted to bid you all adieu."

"Well, adieu to you too, Doc. Boys, this calls for a round on the house."

Johnson lined up a row of glasses on the bar and began filling them, not with the whiskey he kept under the bar, but from one of the fancy bottles lined up along the mirror.

Doc watched the whiskey sloshing into the

glasses, and he began nodding and muttering to himself. He could smell it now, or at least he thought he could, and taste it with his entire being: tongue, sinuses, throat, liver. He desperately wanted a drink.

No! Not another plunge into death. He had alcohol beaten now; he hadn't had a drink in nearly twenty-four hours.

Still, how could he know if he had it beaten if he didn't try just one drink? One probably wouldn't hurt. Then he'd stop. He'd stopped yesterday morning after one, and he could stop now.

"I'll take one of those, Ben," he said, licking his dry lips.

Johnson shut one eye and squinted at the old man. "You sure, Doc?" he said so softly the others couldn't hear.

"I'm sure," croaked Surgeon Raleigh J. Benjamin. "And then maybe I'll buy one for the house."

The sun stabbed through the east window of the shack behind the Silver Dollar Saloon and into Doc's eyes. Half awake, he covered his face with his hands, consciousness flooding him as that first glass of whiskey had flooded him the day before. He couldn't remember anything past that first drink.

He lay on the rough cot, taking stock.

His first impulse was to gag. He'd apparently been smoking cigars, the stale smell woven deep into the wool he was wearing. Sweet Mary, mother of Jesus, he needed a drink. His mouth was dry, and his throat felt as though someone had run sandpaper over it.

It was cold: he was cold, shivering. Then he realized he had wet himself, lain in his bed and wet himself like a baby. Shudders racked him and he wanted to cry, but his body was parched and he didn't have even a few tears left to succor his soul.

His hands probed damp pockets. Nothing! Not a penny left of the money he had needed to return to Atlanta, to live with his brother. At least, he still had the voucher for the tickets. As long as he had that there was hope.

Eyes shut tight against that painful light, his fingers probed his pockets, one after another. Nothing! He didn't have the letter about Emma or the voucher. His old suit! He had left the letter in his old suit!

Charley the barber had picked up Doc's ragtag suit, holding it away from himself in two fingers, nose wrinkled. "I'll burn these for you, Doc," he had said. And Doc agreed, glad to be shut of that piece of his life. But he had left Marcus's letter in that suit! He had no way out now; he would die of cirrhosis in Sanctuary and be buried in a potter's grave.

Doc wailed, a high-pitched keening, his misery leaking from him like blood from a shrapnel wound. He had killed himself, and now he was mourning because no one else would.

"Awake, Doc?" someone called.

Doc forced his eyes open. The preacher was towering above him, black suit drawn sharp in the morning light, face shining in the sun.

"The gold piece was yours, wasn't it?" Doc asked.

The preacher nodded.

"I haven't got it anymore."

"I know."

"Going to throw me in jail, preacher?"

"No, I meant for you to have the money."

Doc shook his head, trying to make his mind work.

"I don't understand."

"You will. But first we have to get you cleaned up. I've got a room for you in the hotel."

Mordecai reached down to help Doc to his feet, but Doc waved him away. He clambered to his feet and lurched to the door, leaning against the frame while he vomited, emptying his belly of all the poisons he had pumped into it.

The next three days were hidden in a haze. Occasionally the fog cleared and Doc could see the hotel room, single bed against one wall, commode and wardrobe against the other, a thunder mug beneath the bed.

But mostly Doc remembered the preacher forcing water into him and cleaning up the mess when he couldn't hold it down, sitting beside the bed in the soft light of the kerosene lamp at night and silhouetted in the sunlight streaming through the south window by day.

Doc had tried to jar himself awake, to make sense of what was happening, but whenever he tried to talk, the preacher told him to sleep, and he would close his eyes and plunge into darkness.

Sleep was a blessing. Gut-wrenching pain had broken his resolve in earlier attempts to shake loose from the bottle. But there was no pain in the deep sleep, only peace splintering into confusion as he edged toward consciousness. The preacher must be giving him a sedative, but Doc couldn't remember taking any.

Doc had been awake now since dawn, trying to put the pieces of his mind back together. He wanted a drink, but he was too weak to walk to the Silver Dollar. And for the first time in as long as he could remember, his belly wanted food more than whiskey.

As his mind mulled that, he heard a rap at the door.

The preacher stepped in, carrying a coffeepot and two mugs. "Thought you might need a cup of coffee."

"What I need is a drink."

"No, what you need is to get yourself straightened out."

Doc glared. "What is it about preachers that makes them think they can poke into your life without invitation?"

"What is it about you, Doc," the preacher replied softly, "that makes you drink yourself senseless so you lay in a shack and wet your pants?"

Doc's face went white.

"You'd drink, too, if you'd been through what I have."

"Tell me about it, Doc. Tell me what you've been through."

And Doc did. He opened himself to the preacher, tentatively at first, as he might have opened a patient's belly in search of a tumor. He told the preacher about Emma. She glowed with life and love, Doc said, and he would have been happy simply to spend his life near her, watching her, warmed by her.

But then, Marcus had won Emma's hand, and Raleigh had fled to the army in 1874, his romantic spirit driving him to the frontier and to the command of Colonel Nelson A. Miles. Miles was tough and resourceful, and Doc admired him greatly until that day in the Bear Paws when the colonel ran Chief Joseph to the ground.

It was man against man for a while, and the soldiers were unable to crack the nut Joseph and his people had set in the Montana mountains just forty miles south of the Canadian border.

So Miles had laid siege to the camp, pounding it with artillery, and when General Oliver O. Howard arrived, the Nez Percés surrendered.

Surgeon Raleigh J. Benjamin had been one of the first into the camp, picking and choosing among the wounded men, women, and children. This one would survive without immediate treatment. This one would die regardless. This one would die without immediate treatment.

There was great pain and blood and hatred and resignation in that camp, and Benjamin strode through it like an angel of the Lord, dispensing life and death.

He spent the next week cutting the limbs from the bodies of infants and children, shutting the eyes of mothers as their children looked on, and treating the wounds of men who had no room in their souls for anything but hatred.

And at the end of that week, Army Surgeon Raleigh J. Benjamin had resigned his commission and buried himself in a bottle. He wasn't sure how long he had wandered before he found Sanctuary, he said. He'd tried to resurrect himself in a practice there, but alcohol and the eyes of those children haunted him, and finally he had hidden, had become a geek, a swamper in the Silver Dollar Saloon.

By the time Doc finished his story he was weeping, tears testament to his lost love and lost life.

"Do you see now why I drink?" he sobbed.

"Yes, I see," the preacher said. "But you don't."

Doc stopped sobbing for a moment, eyebrows raised to give his eyes freedom to range over this man in black coat and clerical collar.

"Doc, you drink because you're a coward. You've run from every challenge in your life. You have taken God's gifts and traded them for the oblivion of alcohol. You're a coward, Doc, pure and simple."

Doc raged at Mordecai, desperately trying to hurt the preacher as the preacher had hurt him, but his fists fell softly as a child's.

Mordecai took the blows without defending himself, waiting for Doc's exhaustion to cool the rage within him.

When the last feeble blows had struck, the preacher said, "Best that you get some rest now," and Doc fell as if he'd been rapped with an axe handle.

He didn't even dream, his mind shut down until the knock at the door nudged him into consciousness. The preacher edged into the room, this time carrying a mug of soup and a pot of coffee.

"Thought you might be ready for breakfast," the preacher said.

Doc glared at the preacher, trying to reconstruct his rage. But the sleep had eased his rancor, and he sighed. "You must have been reading my mind."

The preacher grinned. "Doesn't take much guesswork to figure that a man who's been asleep for three days would want something to eat."

"Three days?"

"That's what the calendar says. You needed to get your strength back."

"How long have I been here?"

"This is the fifth day."

Doc pushed his legs over the edge of the bed and struggled to sit up. "I've got to get moving."

"Where are you going, Doc? Back to the Silver Dollar?"

"Damn you, preacher!"

"Are you going to blame your cowardice on me now, Doc? What will you do when you run out of other people to blame?"

"Leave me alone."

"To die, Doc?"

Doc's eyes jerked around to settle on the preacher.

"I've seen cirrhosis before, Doc. If you don't stop drinking, you're going to die. That's not an easy way to go."

Doc burst into tears. "What can I do?"

The preacher put his hand on the old man's shoulder.

"Doc," he said gently. "You've spent all your life digging a hole. You're down to bedrock now, and you can't go any deeper. The walls are starting to give way, and when they do, you'll be buried down there at the end of a wasted life.

"There's no way you can scramble out by yourself. But if you really want out, all you have to do is ask, and a rope will come curling down from above. You can pull yourself out with that rope. It'll be some work, but you can do it.

"Do you want that rope, Doc?"

Doc nodded, tears erupting again and

streaming down his face.

"Let us pray," the preacher said, taking Doc's hands in his own.

Three

Judd sat on the step in front of his shack, picking pebbles from beneath his feet and chucking them halfheartedly at opportune targets. But his attention was focused on the slaughterhouse, red lead and rough lumber, perched on a knoll above the camp.

The boy had awakened that morning to the crack of a .22 rifle from above: once, twice, three times, four and five. Five steers with bullets in their brains, enough work to keep the meat plant operating all day. By the time he climbed from bed, two of the steers were hanging from a crossbar in front of the building, opened and swaying a bit in the fresh spring breeze.

Judd might have gone up to the slaughterhouse then, but he had heard the low rumble of Jasper's voice. He couldn't understand the words, but he didn't have to. Jasper had only one mood — ugly — and to go to the slaughterhouse now was to . . . Judd shuddered.

Judd's stomach rumbled to protest its emptiness. He and his grandmother had shared the steak the preacher had given him with the Old Hawk family. The Old Hawk children were young and didn't understand hunger yet, so it was best to give them most of the meat.

The steak bone and beans given them by the Old Hawks had taken the edge off, but now his hunger had returned and the time had come to spend the quarter.

Through the cracks in the door behind him Judd heard his grandmother stirring. She would be rising soon, and she would be hungry. It is not easy to awaken hungry and know that you will go to bed hungry, too.

Judd sighed.

Holding the quarter clenched tightly in his hand, he walked up the hill toward the slaughterhouse, but there was no spring in his step and only resignation in his eyes.

Jasper and the others had trimmed around the steer's hind-quarters, and they were trying to strip the hide off the animal, tugging at it like ants tugging a grasshopper back to their hill. Entrails lay in a pool beneath the steer, and occasionally one of the men would step in them, grunting as he slipped.

"Son-of-a-bitch doesn't want to give it up, does he?" one man asked, wiping the sweat from his forehead on a blood-soaked sleeve.

"Probably figures there's still some cold

left this spring," another replied, and the men chuckled, still grunting from the effort.

Judd had walked up behind the group, and he stood there waiting for one of them to notice him, but no one did.

Finally the hide peeled off, prodded along here and there by the fine edge of a knife. The skin was pulled off the animal's neck and draped for a moment over the steer's head, as though the animal were embarrassed by its nakedness.

Jasper grabbed a saw from a nearby table and began cutting the animal's head off. He was through the spine in a matter of minutes and his knife made short work of the rest of the steer's throat.

The men draped the hide, hair down, on a fence. One bent over the animal's head, grunting as he dug the steer's tongue free from its skull. He held it up, gray and rough as a rasp, before dropping it in a galvanized tub with the heart and liver.

The others had stopped for a moment, breathing deeply, their breath painting plumes in the air.

It was then that Judd cleared his throat.

The boy's heart was racing, and even in the cold he could feel a drop of sweat course down his back, but he attempted to carve his face from stone as the men looked up.

"You can count on it, can't you, boys?" Jasper said, "Butcher, and the smell will bring out all the dogs within sniffing distance. Sorry-looking mutt, ain't he."

"I have money," Judd said, holding out the quarter.

Jasper slapped the bottom of Judd's hand, and the coin sailed into the air beyond his reach but not beyond Jasper's. He snatched it like a rainbow trout chasing a stone fly.

"I'll be damned," Jasper said in mock amazement, pocketing the coin. "It can talk, just like it was a real person. What's this world coming to?"

Sniggers rippled through the men. They had watched Jasper play this game before.

"Wonder if this talking dog knows any tricks? You'd think a smart dog like him would know something."

Jasper leaned down and sliced a handful of meat off a fresh liver. He held the meat shoulder high.

"Let's see you beg. Smart dog like you ought to be able to beg."

Judd knew the routine. He tried to turn off his mind, focusing only on the hunger he had seen etched on his grandmother's face. He tried to remember the thin faces and the big black eyes of the Old Hawk children. And then he dropped to his knees, holding his hands in front of him as a begging dog might hold his paws.

"See," Jasper said. "That dog ain't as stupid as he looks. He picked up begging right off. Now, let's see another trick, dog. Let's see you roll over."

The ground was stained with the blood of a thousand steers. Weeds and maggots shared that bloody brew, but Judd did as he was told, his eyes open and staring, seeing only the face of his grandmother.

"Now this is the tough trick," Jasper hissed, and the grin on his face was a terrible thing to see. "This dog's going to have to catch this liver in his teeth, or he's going away empty-handed.

"You understand that, dog?"

Judd kneeled on the ground, his face hard as granite and pale as a winter moon. Tears ran down his cheeks and dripped on his shirt, but he felt nothing, nothing at all.

"That's enough fun," one of the men whispered. "Just give him the meat, Jasper, and we'll get back to work."

But the man wilted under the heat of Jasper's glare, and he stepped back.

"Now, dog," Jasper said, menace poking from his voice like spines from a yucca. "Let's see if you can learn this new trick.

"Let's see if you can catch this liver in

your teeth. Had a dog once that could do that. Throw him a piece of meat, and he'd snap it out of the air like a rattler after a mouse.

"You ready, dog? I'm going to throw it now."

"No, you're not."

The little knot of men jerked around.

"Where in hell did you come from?" one asked. Then he noticed Mordecai's collar and whispered, "Sorry, preacher, for the language."

"The language is the same if I'm here or not."

The men started to break up, but they were pulled back by the harshness of Jasper's voice. "You being a preacher don't mean a damn thing to me," he said.

Jasper had dropped the liver back into the tub and picked up his knife, shining dull and bloodstained. He held the knife low, edge up and pointed at Mordecai's heart. "Suppose you get the hell out of here, and let us get on with our business."

"You've got half your business taken care of," the preacher replied, an edge creeping into his voice. "You took the boy's quarter, and I figure that's worth two livers and a beef heart. Isn't that the going rate?"

Mordecai glanced at the rest of the men.

They nodded, too intent on the drama unfolding before them to speak.

"Seems to me that the 'entertainment' you had at the boy's expense ought to be worth something, too — say a front quarter."

Jasper turned livid. "You're about to get more entertainment than you bargained for," he said, snarling. "Preacher, I'm going to gut you just like this steer here, and hang you up for the whole town to see, collar and all."

Jasper lunged, his knife coming in low and fast and ugly.

The preacher sidestepped, and Judd slipped on the pile of entrails, going down to one knee. When he rose, the preacher was standing behind him, unbuckling his belt.

Jasper grinned malevolently. "Well, look at this, boys. The preacher's afraid he's going to pee his pants."

The preacher waited. Jasper came at him like a bear stalking a wounded deer, and the preacher's arm moved in a blur.

Crack!

Jasper's eyes widened. Two cuts crossed his cheek like wagon tracks. Blood seeped down his face.

Crack! Crack! Crack! Crack! Crack!

The preacher was twirling the belt about his head now, and at each revolution it cut into Jasper's face, neck, arms. Jasper stumbled backward, fleeing the belt as a child flees a nest of aroused yellowjackets.

Crack! Crack! Crack! Crack! Crack!

The knife clattered to the ground, and Jasper followed it, rolling into a ball, arms doubled over his face. His shirt was shredded, blood oozed from him, and he was sobbing. "Please, no more. No more. Please. Please."

The preacher turned to the other men, and they stepped back.

"Turn the other cheek on a man with a knife," the preacher said. "Likely as not, you won't have it."

One of the men twittered, and nervous laughter pattered through the butchers.

"I'm going to be in the Silver Dollar Saloon around nine o'clock Sunday morning," the preacher said. "I'd like to buy all of you a drink."

"I'll be there," said the man who had tried to stop Jasper from abusing Judd, and some of the other men nodded, too.

"Now," the preacher said, "I'd like two livers and a beef heart and a front quarter. You can take the quarter out of Jasper's wages.

"Right, Jasper?"

The heap on the ground moaned.

Judd and the preacher walked toward the camp, the preacher listing a bit under the

57

weight of the beef, and Judd carrying the livers and the heart in an old flour sack they found hanging in the slaughterhouse.

"Why did you come?" Judd asked.

"Just walking," the preacher replied. "And once I was there, I couldn't let him do that to you."

"I didn't see you come," Judd continued, his voice stretched a bit with the effort of carrying the meat. "You weren't there, and then you were."

"There was a lot going on. You just missed me in all the hullabaloo."

Judd's eyes narrowed, and they walked in silence for a few moments.

"Thank you," Judd whispered.

"That's not something I like to do," the preacher said. "But you can't talk to a man like Jasper, at least not when he's on the prod. He shouldn't bother you for a while."

A fire was burning in the dump, and Judd's nose wrinkled. He had lived in that smell most of his life and still he hated it.

"You can leave the meat," Judd said. "I can get help to carry it from here."

"Came this far. Might as well go the rest of the way."

The shacks hung in the haze on the far side of the dump. The Old Hawk children were rummaging through the garbage, looking for toys and anything else they might sell or use. Some of the older people picked through the dump, too, looking for scrap metal and clothing, cast-off goods for cast-off lives.

There were eight shacks, mostly logs accented here and there with mismatched boards of varying colors. Old tubs, buckets, flowerpots, and shovels worn flat and dull from Montana gumbo lay scattered around the buildings. Years of feet had worn the grass away, leaving dirt corrupted by broken glass, tin cans, and toys worn out long before the Indian children had gotten them.

Three men squatted in front of one shack, smoking.

"Don't look at them," Judd muttered quietly, "or they will take this meat and your money." He hesitated a moment. "They might hurt you, too."

Here and there a child's face, nose flattened against a windowpane, peered out at them with eyes too deep and dark to fathom.

Judd and the preacher marched through the tiny village, carrying raw meat and the villagers' attention with them. Judd stopped at the step of one of the shacks, totally unremarkable from the others, and called, in Cree, low and insistent.

"Grandmother, we have meat — and a visitor."

There was stirring inside the shack. Judd and the preacher could hear it in the creak of floorboards and the clatter of something inadvertently kicked, skittering along the floor. Judd waited a long moment, then opened the door.

Grandmother was sitting in the rocking chair where she spent most of her time. Later, as the sun warmed the Montana prairie, she would move it outside, sitting in the sun as her hands moved by memory over one project or another.

The old woman was as wrinkled as her clothing, and it seemed in the dim light that they were one, that someone had dropped a bundle of rags on the chair and set them to rocking.

Her eyes, black as a river slough on a summer night, followed the meat to the table, her nose wrinkling. Judd knew that she smelled the meat, and the scent set her belly on edge.

"Grandmother, we are not invisible to him," Judd whispered. "He can see you."

She thought about that a moment, still as a rabbit listening for the quiet pad of a coyote.

"Where did you get the meat?" she asked in Cree, her eyes still on the table.

"At the slaughterhouse," Judd replied in

60

Cree. "The preacher helped me."

"Why did you bring him to our home?"

"He carried the meat."

"That is bad. You should never bring a white man here. There will be trouble now. They will make us go away, and we will be cold next winter. Tell this preacher to go away. Tell him we don't want him here."

The preacher had been standing by the door, listening as the old woman spoke.

"Grandmother," Mordecai said in Cree. "There was a time when the people welcomed visitors. What have I done to offend you?"

The old woman started. Until that moment, it had seemed that her eyes were too cloudy to notice the visitor. Now they probed his face, her mind trying to see past the cataracts that blurred her vision, trying to see past the color of the preacher's skin.

"How is it that you speak Cree?" she asked.

"It is not my first trip to the prairie," he answered. "Nor the first time I have visited one of your people."

"Are you one of the people," she asked, "or a Métis?"

"I am of many people. We are all of many people."

The old woman pondered that for a moment and then nodded. "Yes. That is true. My mother, the boy's great grandmother,

61

was Chippewa. We are all of many people. I apologize to you. You are welcome in our house, and I thank you for the meat you have brought us."

"The meat is Judd's," the preacher replied. "I only helped him carry it."

"Call the Old Hawks and the others," she said, turning to Judd. "We have meat to share."

Clinton Old Hawk came tentatively into the shack, hat in hand. When he saw the meat on the table, he bit his lip. But he stood unmoving, eyes on the meat, mind on the white man standing in the corner of the room, almost at his elbow.

Grandmother Medicine Elk cut a generous portion from the beef quarter and gave Old Hawk nearly half of one liver.

"I have bread," he said in Cree. "Old bread from the back of the bakery. Baker Jamison left it for farmers to feed their pigs, but this time I beat the pigs to it.

"I would share that with you." He grinned, brown, crooked teeth showing from a mouth hidden moments before in the thin line of his lip.

Grandmother's eyes jerked to the preacher.

"He speaks the people's tongue," she said.

Old Hawk's eyes grew round.

"The baker had thrown the bread away,"

he said, his words coming in a rush. "I was stealing only from the pigs."

The preacher shook his head. "I will say nothing of this."

Old Hawk's breath escaped in one long sigh.

"I was told that if they caught me stealing again, I would go to prison. Prison is not bad. There is food every day, but I would fear for my family."

The preacher nodded.

"Did you intend to share the meat with the others in the village, Grandmother?" the preacher asked.

She nodded.

"Perhaps you would tell the others of Grandmother's generosity," the preacher said to Old Hawk. "And perhaps you could tell them that I would like to talk with them after everyone has shared in the meat."

Old Hawk nodded and fled the cabin, his entire being shouting relief.

The squatters were scattered like driftwood in front of the Medicine Elk home. Only the children moved, squealing as they played tag with one another. One boy of about two years held his mother's skirts as though they were the only anchor in a world askew, his eyes boring unashamedly into the preacher's from a face stained with dirt.

The faces were vacant, but Judd knew what they were thinking. They had meat, and now the price was to be paid in the coin of their attention or labor.

The preacher stood before them, his face as unfathomable as theirs, and when he spoke it was in the people's tongue.

"You will eat now of the meat that Judd and his Grandmother gave you and of the bread Clinton Old Hawk and his family shared. But the day after tomorrow, the pain will crawl into your bellies again, and your children will cry themselves to sleep.

"Only you can chase the hunger away, but I can show you how. Together, we can fill your children's bellies. What do you say?"

"I say you're full of bullshit." One of the three toughs, whiskey bottle in hand, stood on the edge of the group, swaying a little. "I say you come not for the people's need, but for your own."

Judd's breath hissed through his teeth. Jack Ten Horses terrorized the village. He survived by stealing from the people and by rolling drunks as they staggered away from Sanctuary saloons. It was said he had killed Billy White Man in a drunken brawl by the river, but never said to his face.

Ten Horses, thick bodied and bandy

legged, malevolence and alcohol painted across his face, stood with his hands on his hips, glaring at the preacher.

"Speaking the tongue is a trick, like all the tricks the white man plays on the people. You are here now for yourself, not for these," he said, dismissing the squatters with a wave of his hand.

He went on, "You are here to serve your own conscience, not the bellies of the people. And once you have done that, you will walk away, your feet crushing into the dirt the hope you have planted here, and we will be left here to watch it wither away."

Ten Horses spat on the ground, his face grimacing from a bitter taste in his mouth.

"Go now, preacher. Go now, or I will kill you and feed your body to these people you care so much about."

A murmur ran through the crowd.

Judd stepped forward. The cold spring sun sparkled against the sweat glistening on his forehead. He knew Ten Horses as only few in the village did.

As a boy, Ten Horses had trudged up the hill to the slaughterhouse, chosen to sacrifice his pride so that those waiting below — too frightened and proud to go — might eat. He had barked and begged and rolled over for Jasper, and he had learned to hate as few did.

Then one day Ten Horses left the village without looking back; he lived only in rumors. He had been seen in the Bear Paws. He had killed White Man in a drunken brawl.

Cold and hunger lay on the village that first winter like death. The people waited until Judd's grandmother, tears in her eyes, sent Judd trudging through the snow to the slaughterhouse and Jasper.

When Ten Horses returned, face hard and scarred as chipped flint, he bullied the village as Jasper had bullied him. But he didn't bother Judd or his grandmother, honoring a bond Jasper had forged between them, as much bond as either would allow.

But now Judd felt compelled to speak on behalf of the preacher, and that would make Ten Horses his enemy and life even more difficult.

"Wait," he said, his voice cracking. "You must know. The preacher just whipped Jasper."

Another murmur swept through the crowd, only louder this time.

Ten Horses cocked his head, looking at the preacher from the corners of his eyes. He hated Jasper, but he feared him even more.

"How did he whip Jasper?" Ten Horses whispered.

"With his belt," Judd said. "Jasper pulled

a knife, and the preacher whipped him until he fell to the ground, bleeding like raw meat."

"*Hai-eee,*" Ten Horses howled. "How I would have liked to have seen that." He wrapped himself in his arms then, his chin resting on one fist and his eyes hard on the preacher. "I will do nothing now. But remember that when you decide to abandon my people, I will be waiting. Then we will see."

The air hissed out of Judd's lungs like steam from one of the great train engines.

"For now," the preacher said, "all I ask of you is that you collect jars, all the jars you can find. I will be back within a week.

"Also I have found a doctor for you. I will bring him with me next time I come."

The preacher turned and put his hand on Judd's shoulder. "Now, I want you to show me to the newspaper office."

Four

A bell tinkled over the door as the preacher stepped into the rattle and clatter of a flatbed press in the *Sanctuary Bugle*.

Ben Topple — editor, publisher, bookkeeper, swamper, reporter, and printer for the paper — stood beside the press, scrutinizing an auction poster. He waved absently without looking up.

The preacher stood in the entryway, an uncluttered patch of floor in the midst of chaos.

The office was more paper than news. Stacks of the stuff slouched in corners and on tables and sloughed off here and there to lie on the floor like some mad artist's view of life. Topple's desk, covered by a chest-high heap of papers, stood against one wall.

And Topple, wearing a gray and black printer's apron, fitted into the tableau like a headline on a page.

Content with his poster, the printer, a skinny man of about thirty with a perpetual squint, tiptoed across the floor toward Mordecai, stepping from one uncluttered spot to another as though he were fording a stream.

"I'm Ben Topple, owner of this . . . this . . ." His arm described a circle around the room. "Or maybe I should say that it owns me," he said, grinning.

He stuck out his hand, then withdrew it, wiping the residue of thick, black ink on his apron.

"Coffee?" Topple asked. When the preacher nodded, the newsman tiptoed to the back of the room where a pot simmered on the stove. He spent the next five minutes poking through shelves and boxes for his spare cup. He found it in a pile of papers on the floor.

Topple peeked into the cup, and his lip curled. He poured in a little hot coffee and scrubbed the cup with his fingers, foul liquid dribbling on a pile of stained and wrinkled papers at his feet. He squinted into the cup again and, apparently content with his effort, tossed the remaining muck out the back door. Then he wiped the mug with a relatively clean rag hanging from a nail on the wall.

Topple tiptoed back across the room and handed the preacher a cupful of thick liquid the color of a moonless night. Then he leaned his lanky frame against his desk and said, "Figured you'd be in. You've created quite a stir in town, preacher, and it's my guess that you're here to stir the pot some more."

Mordecai grinned.

"Could be."

"Well, what can I do for you?"

"I would imagine that you cover most of the city council meetings?"

Topple nodded.

"Well, I'd like to rent ten acres or so down around the dump to put in a garden. I'm willing to pay, but I need to know who I should approach."

"You saw the shacks?"

Mordecai nodded.

"They're ghosts," Topple said. "I saw them, too. I even imagined walking through that little village and seeing big-eyed children peeking out of dirty windows.

"When I first settled here I wrote an editorial saying it was a darn shame that we had so much and they had so little, and we'd all be better off if we shared with them.

"Got a bushel of letters — most of them saying that if the *Bugle* subscribers wanted to read fiction, they'd buy dime novels.

"Advertising and printing dried up — just dried up — and the papers would be tossed on the back step same day they were delivered."

Topple swept some papers off a chair in

the vicinity of his desk, sat down and continued, "From what I've been able to gather, the good folk here have gotten around the love-your-neighbor principle by deciding that they don't have any neighbors — leastways, none that aren't white.

"Took them a while to cure me of my aberration, but I've seen the light, and I don't see those shacks or those red-skinned ghosts anymore. . . . There might be a lesson in that."

"I just want to rent some land for a garden," Mordecai replied.

Topple cocked his head and squinted at the preacher. He scratched the back of his neck without taking his eyes off Mordecai. "Well . . . Mary Dickens would be most sympathetic, but I don't know what good that'll do you. Mary came here from back east — Connecticut, I think — and got involved in the Women's Christian Temperance Union. When a couple of seats opened on the council, the union decided it was time for a woman councilman. Mary was the only one wasn't married and didn't have a husband weighing her down, so they picked her.

"Although the women in the union couldn't vote, they put posters all around town that said, 'If you don't vote for Mary Dickens, you don't know beans — yet.'

"All the men were laughing about that until they found out what it meant. The ladies served them beans — just beans — morning, noon, and night, for a week. Said if Mary wasn't elected, they'd be eating nothing but beans until they sprouted.

"Men had a big meeting down in the saloon, but wasn't anything they could do about it, so Mary won. Got more votes than the mayor.

"But the first night she took her seat on the council, Mayor Barnaby rose on a point of order. Said that Mary had won fair and square, but since she was a woman, she would not be allowed to vote. You should have seen those women in the audience fume, but — " Topple shrugged.

"So Mary sits on the council, but she can't vote. You wanted the name of someone on the council? She'd be the most sympathetic, but she has about as much influence as those 'ghosts' down by the dump. Mayor Barnaby struts and frets his piece on the stage, but only that. The real push and shove on the council is Anthony Goodnight, but he's one of the marchers in the Reverend Eli's church, and he isn't likely to smudge his soul dealing with haunts.

"I know he won't deal with a 'blasphemer'." The lines in Topple's forehead deepened, and his eyes almost disappeared as he studied the preacher's face. "Didn't take long for that story to get around town.

"Mary'd be your best bet," Topple concluded. "She'd take great pleasure in putting one across on those stiff-necks after what they did to her."

Topple pulled a gold, hunting-cover watch from his pocket. "Mary teaches school. Classes are out in about fifteen minutes. School's on that bluff overlooking the river on the northwest edge of town. She'll either be there or in the teacherage out back — nowhere else for her to go."

Outside, Judd pressed himself against the back wall of the printing shop, willing himself into the pores of the unpainted wood, willing himself invisible.

Time stretched until it sang like a telegraph wire in a winter wind. Why was the preacher taking so long? Why had Judd agreed to wait?

With his ear pressed against the back wall of the *Bugle* building, Judd could hear the rumble of voices inside, but he couldn't understand what they were saying.

A moment ago, the back door of the haberdashery next to the printing shop had opened and the owner dragged a barrel of waste paper into the alley. He had glanced in Judd's direction, but his eyes were empty as the eyes of the catfish the boy sometimes caught in the Milk River.

Still, when the door to the haberdashery closed, Judd could hear the latch click shut. Perhaps the owner sensed that invisible people were about and that his goods were in jeopardy.

Judd shivered. He should have known better than to follow the preacher into such peril. To be in the middle of town in daylight was too risky.

Judd wanted to run, but to run was even more dangerous than to stay. He had tried running once last summer. . . .

The sun sucked energy from the earth that day. The air, heavy as a club, seared the throat and lungs. Only the flies moved, safe from the halfhearted swats of men and the listless swish of cows' tails.

Judd sprawled in the shade of the shack, listening to the creak of his grandmother's chair as she rocked beside him, watching the hills simmer in the distance, breathing the foul pestilence from the dump.

He rolled over on his belly and pushed himself to his knees. The earth spun for a moment, and he reached out to his grandmother's chair to steady himself.

74

"I have to go to the river," he said, and she nodded.

He pulled himself erect and stepped into the heat. He almost retreated; the air, thick and heavy as honey, resisted the passage of mortals.

Judd squinted. The air was warped, the heat so intense that sun and sky and earth merged into one as Judd flowed toward the Milk, slow as the river eddies where the big catfish lie.

His mind oozed out his ears, thoughts light and elusive as flies, and only instinct pulled him from weak shadow to weak shadow until he reached the bank of the Milk. He walked into the water, mud sucking at his feet, aiming to hold him in the sun until he dissolved and became part of the river, flowing toward its reunion with the sea.

A shiver ran over Judd's skin as he sat down on a submerged rock, up to his neck in the cool water. As his body cooled, thoughts began to crackle again across the synapses of his brain. It was then the boy heard the rumble of voices running upstream and against the current.

He had seen the big tent go up the afternoon before and had watched the marchers from the Reverend Eli's church begin their trek toward town, inviting residents to the big revival as insistently as cowboys "inviting" cattle through a gate.

Judd lifted his feet and floated toward the sound, only his face above water, his ears tuned to the click and sigh of a river running slow on a languid afternoon. His eyes watched the sun flash like Thor's hammer through the cottonwood branches overhanging the river.

Judd worried that if someone saw his face floating down the river they might take him for a muskrat and kill him for his pelt. But he was invisible, and anyone waiting on the bank would see nothing but a hole in the shape of his face floating by in the river. He wondered what the people of Sanctuary would think of that. He grinned then, and cool water ran into his mouth, almost choking him.

The great manitou was with him. The spring flood had pulled a cottonwood into the river, but it was still rooted enough in the soil of the bank to remain green-leaved and bushy. Through the green and gray and shadow that was the tree, Judd could see bits and pieces of people standing downstream on the bank. Their lips were moving, apparently in song, but Judd could not hear their voices over the gentle noises of the river.

The river carried him into the cottonwood, and he threaded his way toward the trunk, careful not to shake any branches and reveal his presence, careful not to be swept under the tree and drowned by the current.

Hidden by the tree's foliage, Judd crawled out of the water and lay straddled over a half-submerged limb, peeking through a hole in the branches.

There was a gravel bar below, and three men, one a stranger dressed in black like the Reverend Eli, had waded in waist deep. The others were standing on the bank, singing, sweat glistening on their faces as they swayed with the music.

And then a young woman pulled away from the singers and stepped into the water. Eyes rolling, body shaking, she carried her hands in front of her as though she were blind, her movements jerky as a marionette's.

The Reverend reached for her, and she struggled then, as people sometimes struggle in the night as they awaken from a dream. But the three men laid hands on her and lifted her supine above the water. The evangelist who had come with the tent was shouting something, and so were the people on the bank, but Judd couldn't understand what they were saying and he shook his head to drain the water from his ears.

Then the men thrust the woman beneath the surface of the river, and Judd's eyes grew wide. They were going to kill her, sacrifice her to their God as the Cree sacrificed their pain in the Thirst Dance to the great manitou.

Judd was horrified and fascinated at once. The woman was fighting the men. He could see her body thrashing under the water like a huge fish fighting for its life. And then she stopped fighting and was still.

Judd wanted to scream, but before the sound left his throat, the men pulled the woman from the water. She was limp, her face white and dead, the white robe clinging to her body.

Judd couldn't take his eyes from her face, bleached white in the water. He saw her eyes flicker just before she coughed, a stream of river water flowing back into the Milk.

A chorus of hosannahs and hallelujahs swept the crowd, and the music swelled as the men and women surged into the water to meet their new sister.

There was electricity in the air. Judd could feel it. It tugged at him as it had tugged at the young woman, and he felt compelled, too, to offer himself to the black-robed man, to be sacrificed for his people.

But he knew he wouldn't be welcome there, so he slipped off the branch and into the water, down deep where the current played with the bottom, down where the catfish lie waiting for dead chickens and young boys to come floating by.

Judd felt suspended in time and space, in a world more real and primitive than any he had known. He felt weightless and shameless and sinless, and he tried to hold that, tried to stay in the safety and solace of the cool waters, but his breath hissed out and he was drawn to the surface by his primal need for life.

He broke through the water, gasping for air, and discovered he was alone. The sound of singing pulled his eyes toward the huge tent pitched on the grass in the shade of the cottonwood trees. The assembly from the river was nearing the tent, two of the men holding the arms of the baptized woman, helping her in her disjointed walk toward salvation.

A great shout greeted the people inside the tent, and more than anything in his life, Judd wanted to be part of what was going on there.

He walked out of the river on the trunk of the cottonwood, steadying himself with the branches that seemed always to be where he needed them whenever he began to lose his balance. Water cascaded in sheets from his body, and he shivered a bit in the tree's shade.

On the riverbank, he slipped behind tree

after tree, making his way toward the tent, quiet and cautious. He reached the corner of the tent just as the congregation inside burst into "Onward Christian Soldiers," and Judd was caught in the triumphant strains of the music as certainly as a fish in a net. He stood, his feet shuffling softly against the earth.

And then gently — ever so gently — Judd pulled apart the corner of the tent and peeked inside.

Suddenly the wall of the tent shoved against him. Judd would have fallen, but he was held upright, his wrist caught in the gnarled hand of the Reverend Eli.

Judd struggled as the rabbits struggled in his snares before the thongs took their lives, but he was helpless in the Reverend's grip.

The corner of the tent parted, and Judd was jerked inside, visible: the focus of a hundred eyes and the Reverend Eli's hate.

At first Judd couldn't understand the words. They reverberated through the tent like the boom of a cannon fired in the town park on the Fourth of July. Then he heard, and the words seethed at him, cut him clean as a knife.

"God has sent us a lesson," the Reverend Eli shouted. "There will be many like this sinner who will want to enter the tent of salvation when the end of the world has come.

"But God will reject them, just as I reject this sinner. There is no room for you among believers," the Reverend shouted, shaking Judd by the shoulders. "You are a sinner and the wages of sin is death! . . ."

Judd knew his fate if he were to be caught in Sanctuary without the preacher.

The back door of the print shop scuffed open, and Mordecai stepped through the door, framed for a moment by the unpainted wood.

"Know where the school is, Judd?"

Judd nodded, his eyes probing the alley for ears that might hear the preacher speaking.

"You hold a lot of store in being able to move around without being noticed, don't you, Judd?"

Judd looked at the preacher from the corner of his eye.

"No trick in being invisible, boy." The preacher put his hand on Judd's shoulder, the first time Judd remembered being touched by another person except in anger.

Judd walked stiffly along the alley, aware of nothing but the hand on his shoulder, uncomfortable. But by the time the two reached the end of the alley, Judd felt more at ease.

Judd hesitated before walking into the

street, pulling back against the pressure of the preacher's hand.

"Don't worry, boy. Nobody can see us. We can walk across this street slick as can be as long as we're quiet. You know how to be quiet, don't you, boy?"

Judd nodded. He knew about being invisible. He knew too that it flickered like a candle on a windy night. Sometimes when he most wanted to be invisible — like that time at the revival tent — it didn't work. He didn't want to step into this street now and be paid the *wages of sin*.

But the pressure on his shoulder was firm, and he couldn't resist, so he stepped into the street, his only sound the protest of the dust beneath his feet.

There were a few rigs on the street and some people, but only a horse seemed to notice the two as they crossed. The off-horse on a team pulling a wagonload of cream to the creamery rolled his eyes as he passed and snorted. Muttered curses spouted from the driver, as gray and round as the cans behind. The driver discussed the horse's heritage and future and was still muttering as the rig pulled out of hearing up the street.

When they had reached the darkness and safety of the alley beyond, the preacher whispered.

"Elder in the Reverend Eli's congregation. The good folk of the Church of Righteousness would be surprised that those words crossed his lips. He's mighty careful that no one hears him when he's carrying on like that."

The backs of businesses along Main Street butted against the south side of the alley, but the north half of the block was made up of long, narrow residential lots. Grass and trees in front of most of the homes faded to clotheslines and doghouses and piles of gray, rotting boards in the back. Yet some of the yards were neat, shovels stuck blade deep in gardens almost a month away from seed.

"You can tell more about a person by his backyard than his front," the preacher whispered.

"Quiet, now."

A woman on the long side of sixty slumped in a chair beside a low table that held her washtub and rinse water, sheets snapping on the clothesline in the fresh spring air.

Occasionally her breath would rasp through her adenoids, and jerked awake by the sound, she would stare again at the mountain of wash that she was expected to do.

The woman's chair — back to the alley — was within reaching distance from the fence for a tall man, and the preacher stopped behind the woman, picked up a feather lying in the alley, and drew it lightly across the nape of her neck. She started a bit, her hand moving reflexively to the itch.

The preacher waited a moment and then ran the feather again across the woman's neck. She jerked, hunched up her shoulders, and turned her neck, rubbing it against the muscles of her shoulders. She reached up and scratched her head.

The preacher waited until a tentative snore escaped the woman, and then reached across the fence again. Judd, who had been greatly enjoying the show, could contain himself no longer. Giggles squeaked through his fingers, sounding more like the snort of a pig than laughter.

The woman jerked around just as the preacher dropped the feather and let go of Judd's shoulder.

"You must excuse me, my good lady," the preacher said, sweeping his hat from his head and bowing to her. "I was trying to teach my young friend here the mating call of the bull moose, and I'm afraid we didn't see you sitting there. My heartfelt apologies, madam."

The woman's face was drawn in a knot of suspicion, but it eased as she spotted the preacher's collar. She tried to smile, but the effort was lost to a bone-deep weariness.

"Wasn't sleeping," she said, finally. "Just waiting for the wind to take the moisture from one load."

"That's plain to see," Mordecai said, tipping his hat again.

"We'll leave you to your work, Mrs. Finney. Sorry we bothered you."

They left her staring after them as they walked up the valley, Mordecai saying loudly, "Why don't you try the call, now, Judd?" Judd broke into muffled laughter again, the sound squeezing between his fingers.

"Not bad, my boy. Not bad, at all. Call like that would certainly draw in a lovesick moose." They both laughed then, the sound echoing between the walls lining the alley.

And when they were a block away, the preacher stopped and turned to Judd. "No trick to being invisible. The trick is to make yourself visible. You understand that?"

Judd nodded.

"Wouldn't do now, would it, to have Mrs. Finney turn around to find out she heard a moose call, and not a moose to be seen. She'd be talking about haunts.

"But she'll have a story now that she can share with her neighbors about a preacher man and an Indian boy hunting moose in her alley. She'll have a good laugh over that."

The preacher paused, his voice hardly more

than a whisper. "She deserves another good laugh before she goes."

Judd stared at the preacher as they walked toward the school, but the preacher didn't notice, his mind on other matters.

Five

The school lay a full mile from the edge of town as though knowledge were under quarantine in Sanctuary, but Mary Dickens didn't mind the isolation, preferring it to the company of most of the townsfolk.

And Sanctuary was there when she needed it.

She walked to town on a more or less regular schedule for city council and Women's Christian Temperance Union meetings. When mood and weather meshed, she poked through Sanctuary stores for material for dresses and sewed evenings when she wasn't reading by the light of a kerosene lamp.

On free afternoons when the winter sun was more promise than fraud, she walked through frost-rimed cottonwoods lining the banks of the Milk, enjoying the quiet beauty of the river bottom. But most of her time she spent teaching or worrying about "her" children.

She would see them in the morning walking single file, the older children up front, breaking a path through the snow, the smaller children at the end of the line, bundled as heavily as their bodies and their parents' budgets would allow.

Sometimes she stood on the step of the school and peered into a world turned white. It seemed then that only the school had substance, that to leave it was to step into the void. Then she'd see a vague shape through the whiteout, and one of the older children would appear, ephemeral as a ghost, then the others, hand-in-hand, a train of life trudging through a hostile world.

The children came to school stiff and cut to the bone by the wind, their faces carved stoic and painted red — and sometimes white — by that bitter cold.

It was after one of those days that she had the older boys run rope wings on either side of the school so that the children would not wander past in a storm, dropping one by one as the cold overtook them.

The first minutes of school were spent unwrapping the children and shuffling them swiftly and soundlessly to the potbellied stove glowing red in the back of the room. It was there that she took inventory, determining who was missing and why, checking numb bodies for white or black flesh, sure signs of frostbite.

Miss Dickens had become expert at treating

flesh bitten by those bitter winds. Stricken students were given seats at the back of the room, where they could hide their pain and tears as frostbitten feet warmed in water put on the stove early that morning.

As Miss Dickens faced them from the front of the room, holding tight to the reading book, she tried to drive the children's quiet tears from her mind.

It had been her habit during that first winter to watch for the children as they came to school in the morning and again as they trudged home at night. She didn't know what she could do if windblown snow engulfed her students on their way home, but she watched anyway.

That habit had carried over to early spring, especially after her friend Sarah White explained that spring storms with their soft white flakes were dreaded most by ranchers. Calves and lambs were on the ground and vulnerable.

The children were vulnerable, too, Mary had said, and even though mud was beginning to ooze through the frostbitten soil, she stood in the doorway of the school, watching the children come in the morning and go in the afternoon.

As the children passed a man and a young boy on the trail, Mary caught the flash of white against black. The man was a preacher, tall and slender and wearing a black suit and inverted collar that hung on him like crepe. The boy was a younger version of the preacher, tall and slender, and they both walked easy on the earth.

As they approached, the preacher tipped his hat, the spring sun revealing his face — thin, sun-browned skin stretched tight over fine bones — and Mary wondered for a moment why he had left the warmth of that sun to journey to Montana.

His eyes were brown and warm, belying the hawkish aspect of the rest of his face. He looked, she decided, as a conscripted poet might look in the midst of a long, bloody war.

Mary ran that description past her tongue a couple of times, deciding she would use it in one of the novellas she puttered with in her spare time.

"Mordecai," the preacher said, doffing his hat and holding it across his breast. "This young gentleman is Judd Medicine Elk."

Judd held himself absolutely motionless so that his drab clothing would become one with the raw prairie dirt and the teacher wouldn't see him.

"Mary Dickens," the teacher replied, returning the preacher's grin. "What can I do for you two gentlemen?"

"Wanted to talk to you about renting some city land down by the dump."

"I was about to have tea," Mary said. "Would you like some?"

The preacher nodded, and they stepped toward the teacherage, Judd hanging back.

"Come on, Judd. You can be the chaperon."

"A chaperon isn't needed. It's doubtful my reputation can be damaged any further," Mary whispered as she led the two into the teacherage.

The front room, kitchen, and dining room were all jammed into a space about ten feet square. A huge wood-burning stove dominated the south wall, totally eclipsing a table and two chairs parked next to it. A withered geranium poked from a flowerpot like a sentry posted to watch for the sun.

A rocker with hand-stitched pads on the seat and back stood in the light of the setting sun that eased through the room's only other window.

Mary threw a couple of sticks into the stove, and embers left from its noon feeding licked at the wood as though savoring the taste. Mary moved the rocker over to the table and invited the preacher and Judd to sit down.

Then she bustled around the stove, arranging cookies on a plate and carrying them over to the table.

"Don't wait for me," she said, offering the cookies. "You start and I'll catch up in a minute."

The preacher took one and passed the plate to Judd. The boy shook his head, trying still to be as inconspicuous as possible.

"Take one," the preacher whispered. "You'll hurt her feelings if you don't."

The boy tentatively took one cookie and hid it beneath the table.

"Try it," Mordecai whispered again. "They're good." He punctuated his words by taking a half-moon bite from his own.

The boy studied him for a moment, and then lifted his cookie and bit off a corner. The cookie was crunchy and sweet and good — really good. He stuffed the rest of it into his mouth and reached for another.

The preacher put his hand on Judd's. "Slowly."

Mary sat down, waiting for the teakettle to whistle. "What city land is this, and what do you need it for . . . for what do you need it?" she corrected herself.

"Want to put in a garden down by the dump," the preacher said. "Make a farmer of the boy here."

Mary studied Judd. Her first impression

was the ragged state of the boy's clothing, and the second was his eyes, black and impervious as the obsidian his people once used for arrow points.

"Where do you go to school, Judd?" she asked.

Judd turned his eyes to the preacher, hoping Mordecai would speak on his behalf. But the preacher was silent.

"He speaks English, doesn't he?" Mary asked.

"Sometimes," Mordecai said.

"Where do you go to school, Judd?"

"Don't," he said, his voice little more than a whisper.

"Why not?"

"No school for us."

"No school for Indians?"

"No school for sinners," Judd whispered, his voice tight as his face.

"Why are you a sinner?" Mary asked, her voice soft as the rustle of aspen leaves in a spring breeze.

"The people are heathens," Judd explained, laying his shame before the teacher. "I am of the people."

Rage flared across Mary's face, hotter even than the fire in the stove.

"How could you do that to him?" she hissed, fixing the preacher with a withering stare. "How could you teach him something so — so hateful."

The preacher threw up his arms and leaned back from the force of her words. "I — "

Judd interrupted, "Not the preacher . . ."

As quickly as Mary's temper flared, it changed direction.

"That ugly little man," she said through gritted teeth. "I should have known. It was the Reverend Eli, wasn't it?"

Judd nodded.

Mary stood so fast her chair almost tipped over backwards. She stalked back and forth across the room, her face black with anger.

"That . . . that man!" Mary hissed. "There is no limit to the hate he spews around him."

"He is a man of the cloth," Mordecai said.

Mary turned to glare at the preacher. "He may be a man of the cloth, but he is not a man of God."

"There is a difference?"

"There is a difference." Mary sighed, the anger draining from her. "I didn't mean that as any reflection on you."

Then her temper flared again. "How could he do such a hateful thing to this boy?"

Mordecai shrugged. "Maybe a better question is how could he so control a woman like you?"

"Control me?" Mary raged. "He doesn't control me."

"He isn't even here," the preacher replied, "and still you're dancing on his string."

Mary glared at the preacher and then sighed. "Yes," she said, "I am dancing on his string." She sat down in the rocker, staring out the window, her mind drifting back to that day last fall. . . .

The Jimison boy had been persistent, tugging at her skirt until he pulled her attention away from the other children. That was unusual. Most days he sat quiet as a post, speaking only if asked a question.

He was whispering something, but she couldn't hear his words until she leaned toward him, bending almost double.

"I want to show you something," he whispered. "Outside."

Mary was busy, but this was the first time little Edgar had volunteered anything and she didn't want to discourage him, so she followed the youngster outside.

There, on the bed of a home-built toy wagon, was a rock. "What a nice rock," she said and turned to go back into the classroom, but he caught her skirt again.

"Please," he said.

She knelt beside the wagon. It was a fossil,

an ancient animal encased in rock, and Mary's mind began sifting through some of the paleontology books she had read. A chambered snail about twelve inches in diameter. The rock had split longitudinally and opened the mineralized snail to the wonder of a six-year-old boy and his teacher millions of years after its death.

Her mind settled. Ammonite, from the mesozoic period sixty million to two hundred and thirty million years ago. She reached out in wonder to touch this creature, alive when a sea covered most of Montana.

"This is wonderful, Edgar," she whispered, taking the boy by the shoulder. "Would you mind if we show it to the other children?"

Edgar shook his head, his eyes on the ground, but Mary thought she could see a hint of a smile on his face.

"I found bigger ones," he said. "But I couldn't lift them."

Mary smiled. "This one is just right."

She carried the fossil into the classroom, met by children curious to see what made Edgar's rock different from other rocks. She had told them, then, about the ammonite and how old it was and how it had lived in a time when Montana was covered by a sea. She had pulled one of her books from the sparse bookshelf and was showing the children pictures of some of the animals that were once found in Montana.

Naomi Parkman, classroom tattletale and daughter of one of the elders of the Reverend Eli's church, was standing away from the circle of fascinated children, hands on hips and head tilted to one side.

"That's a lie, teacher."

The other children gasped.

Mary looked up. "Whatever do you mean, Naomi?"

"That rock isn't sixty million years old. God created the earth six thousand years ago. It can't be any older than that."

Naomi was smirking. "You're lying, teacher."

"Where do you think the snail came from, Naomi?"

"I don't know. But I do know it isn't more than six thousand years old. Maybe the devil made it," she said, squinting her eyes at Mary. "Maybe you're a servant of the devil."

Mary gasped, and then ire rose in her throat. "That's enough!" she said. "You go home. I expect you to bring your parents tomorrow, and I expect an apology. Go!"

Naomi stopped at the door and sneered at Mary. "You're going to be sorry you did this. Real sorry."

Naomi did come the next day with her parents, walking side-by-side with the Reverend Eli at the head of his Christian soldiers.

They circled the school as though to prevent Mary's escape, singing verse after verse after verse of "Onward Christian Soldiers" until they were evenly spaced in a ring around the teacherage.

Then the Reverend Eli stepped forward, his face twisted, warped with the fires that burned within him. He placed one shaking hand on Naomi Parkman's shoulder.

"Mary Dickens, you have sinned, and we have come to save you from the fires of eternal damnation."

The Reverend's voice came from deep within his bowels, and the sound echoed off the teacherage and through the river bottom.

"You have been a false teacher, twisting the mind of our dearly beloved and sinless child. You have turned your face from God. Behold the word of God!" The preacher raised his Bible over his head, stretching as though he intended to reach into heaven.

The chanting began then, hallelujahs and hosannahs rippling through the crowd. Mary watched from the shadow of the teacherage, gaping as excitement built in the crowd.

They were moving now, Christian soldiers lost in a rising chorus of chants, reason lost in the mob. One young man, eyes wide and wild, sprinted from the crowd to Mary's door. He swung his fist as though he meant to break the door down. The door shuddered under the onslaught, and Mary could see blood splatter from the young man's fist as he swung again and again.

But there was no pain on his face, no emotion, no humanity. He was dancing on the Reverend Eli's string, an obscene ballet of abandonment.

The Reverend's face seemed forged of molten rock spewed red and black from the earth. When he stepped toward the house, his body was shaking, each step taken as though he were barefoot on broken glass.

"Mary Dickens," he growled. "We have come to offer you forgiveness." A shudder racked his body. "Show us that you repent your sins."

The Reverend's eyes glowed hot as coals, red as the eye of an animal caught in the light of a lantern.

"Come on, Mary Dickens, as that sinner came to Christ in the Pharisee's house, and wash my feet with your tears and dry them with your hair . . . and I will forgive you."

The Reverend's eyes glazed, his fists clenched, and deep shudders ran through his body. Another chorus of hosannahs rolled through the crowd.

But only Mary had been facing the preacher, and only she knew what he meant when he whispered, "Alleluia."

"This sinner is not repentant," the Reverend shouted a moment later. "We must now devote our attention to our own needs. Get behind me, good people, and we will march back to town in the name of the Lord."

Mary watched through the window until the Reverend and his marchers disappeared into town. She wet a towel at the sink and stepped outside to scrub the young man's blood from her door.

She spent more time at it than necessary, her thoughts dwelling on the growing realization that her first year of teaching at Sanctuary would be her last. The Reverend Eli would see to that.

A tear ran down her face and dropped on the step. She would miss her children.

Her thoughts were tugged back, then, even further to that first day. What a commotion she had created when she stepped off the train!

School trustees and their wives and children had turned out in their finest to view this strange creature, a Connecticut woman with a list of degrees after her name.

They had meant to be patronizing, to guide

the "poor thing" clear of the shoals that rippled under the surface of Sanctuary, to help her find her rung on Sanctuary's social ladder.

But when Mary appeared on the train platform, they acted more like a doddering court gathered to pay homage to a princess. She was dressed in the height of fashion, and from the number of male faces pressed against the glass of the car in which she had been riding, it was obvious she had been the focus of attention on the train.

She stood for a moment at the step of the car, as though wondering whether she should climb back aboard. Pretty she was, with light auburn hair and the clear, almost translucent complexion of her Irish background. Shanty Irish, the trustees had said, nodding to each other as they read her application.

But when she spoke at the railroad station, it was apparent that Mary Dickens was a creature of culture and breeding, more of the lace-curtain variety. The men crowded around her, eager to carry her baggage to the buggy provided her.

When she was elected to the city council, the Reverend Eli's congregation was incensed. That Mary Dickens acted more like a man than a woman, they whispered. Could be that she was one of those "transvestites," they hissed, and the men winked at one another when they heard that.

Gossip would likely have eventually cost Mary her job, but she'd hoped that she could spend at least a couple of years in Sanctuary. She was fascinated with the West, as foreign to her as an African veldt, and she wanted to see it, touch it, understand it.

Not much chance for that now. . . .

Mary sighed, and the sigh carried her out of her reverie and back to the table in the teacherage with Mordecai and Judd.

"I will help you get that land," she told the preacher. "I cannot ask directly, of course. The council opposes everything I suggest, so I will have one of my friends ask to lease it, then I will oppose the request. The men on the council will all grin at each other and vote for the lease, to teach that back-east schoolteacher — as they call me behind my back — a thing or two about Sanctuary politics." She smiled wanly. "But you will have your land, and Judd can learn to be a farmer."

Mary put her hand on the boy's shoulder, and he jerked.

"Whose string are you dancing on now, Mary?" Mordecai asked.

Mary's eyes flashed. "My own."

The preacher's voice dropped to little more than a whisper.

"Then I have still more to ask of you," he said. "As I understand it, your contract was for a full year?"

Mary nodded.

"So even though you will not be returning next year, you could stay in the teacherage this summer?"

"I suppose I could, but why would I?"

"I would like you to teach Judd and some of the other Indian children reading and writing and arithmetic."

"Taught to the tune of a hickory stick," Mary whispered, "the way the Reverend Eli says it should be done?"

"No," the preacher said, placing his hand over Mary's. "Taught with love. The way you know it should be done."

Mary looked at the preacher, and her eyes filled with tears. "I would be happy to do that, preacher. Very happy to do that."

Six

Doc sat in a room lit only by a sliver of morning light squeezing past the shade. He was trying hard to ignore the rapping at the door.

But his visitor was insistent, and finally the old man sighed soul deep and croaked, "Come in."

The door opened, and the preacher stood silhouetted in the doorway, black on white like an overexposed photograph. Doc squinted against the light, trying to read the preacher's face, then dropped his eyes, rubbing them with his fingers.

"Figured you'd be around."

"You figured right."

"Wasting your time if you're here to give me a pep talk. Just wasting your time."

"Feeling a little down, Doc?"

Doc sighed. "Yeah. You almost had me there for a while, preacher. I really thought that I could be something that I'm not. But the fact is that I'm a damn good drunkard, the best drunkard this town has ever seen." Tears were running down Doc's face, falling on the table next to the kerosene lamp. "I'll never be anything more than that."

The preacher took Doc by the arm, forcing him to his feet. "No, Doc. That's not what you are. I'll show you what you are. I brought your bag. It's all stocked and ready to go."

"No!" Doc's eyes were wild, crazy. "No! I can't do that anymore. Didn't you hear me? That's what I've been trying to tell you."

The preacher grabbed Doc's shoulders, and looked the old man full in the eyes. "Come with me, Doc. Come with me, and I'll show you who you are."

There was something compelling in those eyes and something compelling in the promise too. So even though Doc was shaking his head, he let himself be pulled from the room for the first time in more than a day.

The preacher led the old man down the back stairs, holding his arms to steady him.

"Where are we going?"

"We'll be there in just a few minutes. Just a stretch of the legs from here."

Doc sidled toward the Silver Dollar Saloon's back door as much from habit as anything as they passed it in the alley. But the steady pressure of the preacher's hand on his arm would not be denied, and he followed, curious now.

They threaded their way through puddles

and patches of mud that defined the streets and alleys of Sanctuary, past backyards still littered with the bones of winter — the spring sun not yet strong enough to pull most people from their homes for spring cleanup.

Doc hadn't walked any distance for years, his only exercise swamping the Silver Dollar. He found the walk tiring but exhilarating too. The spring sun felt strong on his face, and once his eyes had accustomed themselves to its brightness, he saw the town with the clarity spring and fall bring to Montana.

He could hear the spring song of the chickadee — *cheeee-cheeeee* and the cry of the downy woodpecker. And once he saw the flash of a flock of bluebirds in their roller-coaster flight.

It was spring, all right. Still there could be snow — Doc had been snowed on every month of the year in one part or another of Montana — but the promise of warmer times was written on the land.

The two passed the slaughterhouse, choosing the road that bumped down off the bench to the river bottom and the town dump. The road was relatively steep, and Doc's attention was focused mostly on safe places to put his feet, but a flash of white beside the road caught his attention.

Doc pulled loose from the preacher's grip

and stepped across a sidehill to a little ridge open to the full rays of the sun. He stood there for a moment before kneeling on the hillside.

"First one of the season," he said as the preacher stepped up beside him. The old man was pointing to a wild crocus, its silky blossom hugging the ground as though for warmth.

"Haven't seen one in years," he said. "Just haven't been away from the . . . the bottle long enough to look, I guess.

"Early spring is so drab and gray and dead. I think God made these crocuses to bloom now just to show us the promise of color and beauty and life in this land."

Doc stood, but still his eyes were focused on the chip of color. "I've always hoped that when I die, they'll bury me someplace where these crocuses grow."

The preacher put his hand on Doc's shoulder. "Count on it," he said, with a certainty that pulled a smile to the old man's face.

"You know something I don't?" Doc said with a grin.

"Maybe," the preacher answered, a grin spreading across his face too.

They walked down the hill and into the Indian village, a smile painted as tentatively across the old man's face as the crocus was painted on the hillside.

A knot of children stood outside the Old Hawk shack. The younger were playing games in the dirt and mud, but the older children were quiet and vigilant.

Judd was the first to notice Doc and the preacher. He met them in the middle of the village.

"Connie Old Hawk is sick," Judd said, "really sick. She's got a fever, bad, and her stomach hurts. Everyone thinks she will die."

"Doc, here, might have something to say about that," the preacher said.

Doc stopped cold. "No! I'm not ready for something that serious. Not with a child."

"You don't know how serious it is until you see her. Can't hurt to take a look."

The Old Hawks were huddled over the only bed in the room when Doc, the preacher, and Judd stepped in. They looked up for a moment, their faces etched with concern, and then returned their attention to Connie.

The child was flushed with fever, her face glowing red with the fire that raged within her. Mrs. Old Hawk was replacing a wet washcloth on the girl's forehead, but it was obvious that the cloth was as much to treat the helplessness Mrs. Old Hawk felt as Connie's fever.

Connie was about seven years old. Her

normally bright eyes were opaque with sickness. She looked at the two white men dully, without interest.

Doc's breath left him in one long sigh.

He pulled down the blankets on the bed. She began shaking as the fever's chills spread across her body, and Mrs. Old Hawk tried to cover the girl again.

Doc shook his head. He pulled up the girl's shift. Her abdomen seemed swollen and tight and when his fingers probed the lower right quadrant of her belly, Connie cried out in pain.

"Jesus!" Doc said, a light sweat breaking out on his forehead. "Appendicitis. Acute appendicitis. Hard to say how bad it is until the surgeon goes inside, but it looks bad, really bad."

The Old Hawks couldn't understand the doctor's words, but they understood the expression on his face and the tone of his voice.

Mrs. Old Hawk began to keen, and the high-pitched wailing cut into Doc's mind like a razor. He grabbed his forehead with both hands, his knuckles white with the pressure, as though only his fingers were holding his mind in his skull.

Dark thoughts about those days in the Bear Paws when he had been treating Indian children riddled with Army shrapnel came back to him with the fury of a winter storm, and he nearly buckled under the pressure. The Nez Percé women had been keening then, too, while their children died, while Doc fought futilely for their lives.

"Stop her! Please stop her!"

The preacher touched Mrs. Old Hawk's shoulder. She looked deeply into his eyes and found comfort there. He was speaking softly to her in Cree when Doc cut in.

"This girl's got to go to Doctor Wilson's surgery."

"Doctor Wilson was called out to the Grotbo place," the preacher said. "Mrs. Grotbo's due for her seventh, and she's having some problems. He won't be back in town until tomorrow, maybe later."

"You sure as hell know a lot about what's going on in his town," Doc said.

The preacher shrugged. "It's a small town. Hard to keep secrets here, but we couldn't move Connie even if Doc Wilson was here. She'd never survive the trip to the surgery. It's up to you, Doc. It's all up to you."

"No!" Doc's eyes were wild, crazy. "No! You can't ask me to do that. It's been too long, and I'm not ready."

"Doc, this little girl will die unless you get hold of yourself. You're the only hope she has. Maybe that isn't fair, but that's the way it is. Are you really going to let her die just because you're afraid?"

Doc's voice died to a whisper.

"Preacher, I have no great faith in your God," the old man said, his face white as spring snow. "But you best pray for this little girl now as you have never prayed before. Pray for me, too, preacher. Pray for me."

Doc opened his bag. It was fully stocked, as the preacher had promised, including tin cans of chloroform, a half dozen pairs of rubber gloves, antiseptic, gauze, cotton, and what looked to be a full complement of new surgical tools.

His mind was in turmoil, but as he checked through the bag, old procedures and habits came back to him and almost unconsciously he began planning the surgery as carefully as a general plans a battle.

"You ever worked in a hospital, preacher?" Doc asked.

Mordecai shook his head.

"Well, you've managed to acquire everything we need for surgery. That's nothing short of remarkable."

The old man squinted at the preacher, his brow wrinkled in conjecture.

"You told me you were a surgeon," the preacher said. "I asked a pharmacist to stock the bag the way a surgeon would want it stocked."

"No pharmacist in Sanctuary."

The preacher shook his head. No, there was no pharmacist in Sanctuary.

A feeble groan jerked Doc's attention back to the child. Concentrate! He had to concentrate, put everything out of his mind but this young girl's feeble struggle for life.

"Preacher, tell the parents that Connie is very, very sick, and that her only hope is an operation. Explain to them that we will have to cut into that little child's body — here, now."

Doc's voice almost broke then, but he regained control. "If they don't give me permission, I cannot operate, and Connie will surely die. And tell them," he said, his voice dead as stone. "Tell them that she may die anyway."

Doc cleared the table of dishes. He washed it carefully with soap and water, scrubbing it with a brush he found in his bag.

"I'll need a good kerosene lamp, Judd. Not the kind with the wick, but the kind with the mantles. A two-mantle lantern would be nice. It has to be in good working condition, boy. If we lose the light — " Doc left that sentence hanging like dread in the air. "Can you get one for me?"

Judd nodded and stepped through the door,

shoving to get past the crowd outside. Jack Ten Horses had such a lamp. He used it for poker games that stretched long into the night.

Judd rapped at Ten Horses' shack. No one answered, but Judd could hear stirring inside. He rapped again, more loudly. The sound was greeted by a snarl.

The stories about Ten Horses, how he had killed one of his own people, flooded into the boy's mind, and he shuddered but he rapped again at the door.

A dirty curtain hiding the interior of the shack from Judd's eyes was torn aside, and Ten Horses' face, squinting against the light, glared at him.

Judd swallowed hard as he heard the door bolt *snick* open like the bolt of a rifle closing on a cartridge.

"What the hell you want, boy?" Ten Horses growled.

"I would like to borrow your lamp," Judd said in a rush. "The doctor has to operate on Connie Old Hawk, and he needs the light to see."

"Came down to moccasin flats to do some cutting, huh?" Ten Horses hissed. "Could be I'll do some cutting of my own."

He stood, pulling on a pair of trousers and slipping on a shirt.

"We'll see who's bull goose around here,"

he muttered to himself.

Ten Horses was in an ugly mood, and Judd longed for invisibility, but he couldn't forget Connie Old Hawk's fever-stained body and the fear in the old doctor's eyes.

"Can I take the lamp?" Judd asked.

Ten Horses glared at the boy, but nodded.

Judd followed in Ten Horses' wake as he stalked across the little village toward the Old Hawks' shack, cutting through the crowd outside like an axe through kindling.

The butt of his palm slammed against the edge of the door and it split, swinging inside to slam against the wall. Doc was still bent over the table, cleaning it now with carbolic acid.

Both men looked up as Ten Horses crashed through the door, and in the stunned silence Judd heard the preacher say, "Well, Doc, here's the third member of the surgical team and right on schedule, too."

Ten Horses' face traversed the emotional gamut from rage to incredulity.

"Not me," he said, his voice tinged with disbelief. "I'm not going to help you cut into this child. If I do any cutting around here, it won't be on this little girl."

"No," the preacher said. "You're not going to do any cutting. You're going to help us save her life."

"Bullshit!" Ten Horses stood beside the table shaking his head. "I'm not helping you. I don't owe you anything. I don't owe her anything. I don't owe any of these people anything.

"Any debts I had were paid up at the slaughterhouse, and I didn't get so much as a thank-you. I've done my share, preacher. No more. From now on I take, and they give."

"You're going to help give this child life, Jack. I have to help Doc with the retractors. We need a man on the chloroform, and you're elected.

"Judd's the only other one here who speaks English well enough to do it. That's too much of a load to lay on a twelve-year-old. You're going to do it, Jack, because you owe it to yourself."

Ten Horses' bluster ebbed. "I can't. I can't watch while he does that."

"You'll be too busy to watch. You'll be deadening that little girl's pain. You know how to do that. You've probably had more experience at deadening pain than anyone. You have to do it, Jack, if not for her then for yourself."

Doc settled the debate. "Hot water on the stove," he said. "Shed that shirt and wash up. Scrub your body from the top of your head to your belt. Get with it. We haven't

115

got much time."

Jack Ten Horses turned dutifully to the stove.

Doc stood over the little girl, scalpel in hand. He was talking to himself, talking his way through the operation. The preacher and Jack Ten Horses were listening to every word, their consciousness stretched tight.

Ten Horses had never felt so frightened — or so alive.

"I'll be making a McBurney's incision, about four inches long," Doc said. "I expect the appendix is perforated. That will give the preacher and me a little more working room."

The scalpel was trembling in the old man's hand.

"Jesus, I wish I had a drink," he whispered.

The girl was already unconscious, free of pain for the first time in the past several days, unaware she was sole possessor of the minds of the three men and a boy in the squatter's shack, unaware that the entire village waited outside for news of her.

Doc had made a pad of cotton and gauze and showed Ten Horses how to drip the chloroform on it and when. The preacher had given Ten Horses his watch so that he could time the drips, and Doc had shown him how to take Connie's pulse, told him to report any fluctuations.

The preacher stood ready to staunch the first flow of blood when the knife touched belly, and still Doc hesitated.

"Pray for us, preacher," he said, and his hand, steadier now, cut through the skin stretched tight over the girl's swollen belly. The skin opened wide and filled with blood.

Ten Horses turned his head and began to cough.

"You vomit in here and I'll remove your appendix the hard way," Doc growled. "I told you not to watch what I'm doing. You've got enough to do."

And then, almost as an afterthought, he added, "You're doing fine. She didn't feel a thing."

"Damn little fat," Doc said, suturing two bleeders, talking himself through the procedure. "I'm cutting now through the fascia — a thin protective sheath of the external oblique muscle, incising it parallel to the direction of the fibers.

"More bleeders. I'm tying them off now."

Similarly, Doc cut through the internal oblique muscle and then the transversalis, giving the preacher and Jack a running account of each step of the operation.

"This is taking longer than it should,"

Doc said. "The longer I'm in, the harder it is on her."

"You're doing fine, Doc," the preacher said.

The little girl stirred on the table.

"Damn it, Jack! Tend to your business. She's coming around."

Ten Horses dripped more chloroform on the pad over Connie's nose.

"Sorry, it's just hard not to watch what you're doing, and when I do . . ."

Doc broke in again. "Now comes the tricky part." He had reached the peritoneum, a paper-thin lining of the abdominal cavity. Carefully, very carefully, he worked the flexible tissue away from the muscle and down into the wound until it bulged like a balloon into the abdominal cavity under the pressure of his fingers.

"A slip here, and we have a hole in an intestine and we can say goodbye to Connie."

Doc's face was pale, his attention focused solely on the scalpel in his hand and the intestine's natural inclination to spill out of any hole in the abdominal wall.

"Judd, we're going to need that lamp a little closer here in just a minute."

Judd moved closer to the table, holding the light shoulder high and trying to look everywhere but at the gaping wound in front of him.

Doc touched the scalpel to the peritoneum, ever so carefully. He was into the body cavity now, and the primal smell of viscera filled the little shack.

"Now we need the retractor to hold the incision apart, so we can see what's going on there. Tip the light a little, Judd. There. That's just right."

"Jesus!" Doc sagged against the table, and the preacher moved against him, giving him his body to lean on. Doc took a deep breath and began talking again.

"Infection. Bad infection." The words were toneless, bodiless. "It's localized. I take the appendix, and I may spread the infection to the rest of the abdominal cavity and Connie will die.

"I don't take the appendix and the infection will likely spread, and Connie will die.

"Damned if I do and damned if I don't."

He stood for a moment slumped against the preacher and then straightened a little with resolve.

"Give me one of those tubes. We'll drain the abscess first," he decided. That done, Doc began a purse-string suture about a quarter of an inch above the base of the appendix pointing up at him through the wound like an ugly, accusing finger.

Doc was stitching around the base of the

appendix without breaking through its wall and spreading fecal material into the wound.

"That's some fancy stitching, Doc," the preacher said. "You should have been a seamstress."

"Times like this I wish I had," Doc retorted. He cut off the blood-bearing meso-appendix, crushed the base of the appendix above the purse-string suture, tied it tightly, and clamped it above that stricture. The wound was lined with gauze pads, and Doc cut through the offending organ, lifting it carefully through the wound.

He dabbed the stump with tincture of iodine and removed the gauze pads.

Then Doc pushed the stump inside the large intestine and pulled the purse-string suture tight. The effect was to close off the wound, leaving the intestinal wall smooth, and the stub inside.

He left a drain in the abscess, sutured the peritoneum, and stitched up the ugly slash on the belly of the little girl. Then and only then did the sigh that had been building in him since that first touch of the scalpel escape his lips.

"You've got a fine pair of hands, Doc. As good as any I've ever seen."

The hint of a smile on Doc's face evaporated a second later, cut off by Ten Horses' frantic announcement. "She hasn't got a pulse, Doc. Her heart has stopped beating."

"No!" Doc's denial cut through the room like the keening of Connie's mother an hour before. "No! She can't die. She can't."

Doc pressed his ear to the little girl's chest — silence.

Behind him he could hear Judd, the catch in the boy's voice: "When her little brother, Boyd, died last year after he stepped on that rusty can, Connie said she thought she would go visit him so he wouldn't be lonely.

"Is that what she's done? Has she gone to visit Boyd?"

"No!" Doc was denying the little girl's death, pushing on her sternum, willing her heart to beat again. He dropped his ear to her chest — nothing.

The keening began outside the shack, Connie's mother reacting to a sixth sense that ties mothers and their children together. Other women joined in, and Doc was fighting panic.

The preacher stepped past Doc. He cupped Connie's head in his left hand, making the sign of the cross on her forehead. Then he laid his right hand across her forehead and looked up at the other men.

His face was shining as Connie's had shone with the fever burning inside her.

"Join hands," he said. "Form a circle. You too, Judd."

Ten Horses was shaking his head. "None of that mumbo jumbo for me."

But even as he spoke it was obvious that he was fascinated by the preacher, as a bird is fascinated by a snake. And when Doc reached toward him, Ten Horses took the old man's hand in his own and reached for Judd.

"Doc, you put your free hand on me. You, too, Judd." They stood then, a little circle of life in a tarpaper shack, joined together by their love for a tiny, helpless girl they hardly knew.

Life trickled through that circle like electricity through a wire. Each of them could feel it tingling in their hands and arms and hearts. The preacher was speaking, but they couldn't hear his words. They could only "feel" his voice, feel the words crackling across the synapses of their nerves.

And then it was over, and they found themselves standing in that same circle, and at the center of it was a little girl, a little girl stirring and making mewling sounds as she might have made as a baby.

The shout of the crowd roared into the shack and their consciousness, and Connie's mother and father burst through the door, their faces shining with the miracle of a little girl's life.

And when Doc and the preacher and Ten Horses and Judd stepped — still stunned — outside the shack, the crowd parted and stood silent as they passed.

As Doc and the preacher walked up the hill toward the slaughterhouse, the preacher was speaking, but the words pattered off Doc's consciousness like raindrops off a tin roof.

"You're not the 'best damn drunkard' Sanctuary has ever seen," the preacher said. "You are a man with the God-given talents of a fine mind and sensitive hands. You are a man who can make little girls well, offer hope to people who have never dared to wish for anything so grand.

"Your gifts are too precious to be wasted, Doctor Raleigh Benjamin. You are obligated to use them to help the less gifted around you."

Doc stopped and turned to stare the preacher full in the face. "You've told me who I am, preacher. Now, tell me who the hell you are."

"Name's Mordecai," the preacher said. "Just call me Mordecai."

Seven

The Sunday morning crowd at the Silver Dollar Saloon had grown, more from curiosity than anything.

The bar was lined with the backs of men in quiet conversation, most of them drinking coffee from the big pot Ben Johnson kept on the back bar. Three or four of the tables were filled, and a scattering of loners poked up at others.

They all looked up as Mordecai pushed through the heavy front door, faces bobbing around as word of his coming passed along the line of men.

Mordecai nodded and stepped up to the bar. He held up three fingers, and Johnson produced a glass and filled it three fingers deep with whiskey.

"Haven't seen Doc, have you?" Johnson asked. "Miss the old coot."

"He's taken up with Doc Wilson, now, helping out in the surgery. Wilson was impressed with the work Doc did on little Connie Old Hawk. Said he had never seen better."

Johnson shook his head in disbelief.

124

"Who would have thought he had that in him? All those years swamping this place, and he turns out to be a real surgeon. Never know, do you?"

Mordecai shook his head.

"Haven't found anyone to take the job, so I've been doing it myself," Johnson said, his face wrinkling. "Wasn't paying him enough for what he was doing."

"You were paying him more than he thought he was worth."

Johnson shrugged and hurried off to refill a cup of coffee. When he returned, he leaned across the bar, resting on arms locked at the elbows. "If he cuts as good as he swamps, I guess I wouldn't mind him working on me."

"He cuts better," Mordecai said. "Have any port?"

Johnson reached under the bar. "Ordered in two bottles special for you," he said. "All the stories going around, I figured you'd draw a crowd."

When Mordecai reached in his pocket, Johnson shook his head. "The wine's on me. Little enough for me to do. But I would favor a drink same as everyone else."

The preacher smiled. "You're entitled."

Mordecai, serving wine for the last of the men, felt a cool breeze as the front door opened. He felt, too, the tremor that ran through the men as they looked up.

He continued down the line, saying, "Take and drink. This is my blood shed for your sins," ignoring the order that rumbled from the bar.

"Preacher, I want to talk to you" — and later, more insistently — "Preacher, get your rear end over here. I said I wanted to talk to you."

Mordecai finished serving the wine and then stood. He raised his right hand and offered the benediction. Only after he was finished and the men were rising self-consciously from their knees did he turn his attention to the bar.

Jasper was there — the cuts from Mordecai's belt marking his face like a road map — and an older man.

The other man didn't wear his rank. He might have passed for any of the old cowboys in the bar if not for a back straight as a wagon spoke and a bite in his voice that said he was more accustomed to giving orders than to taking them.

As Mordecai neared, he could see the lines cut into the man's face by summer suns and winter blizzards. His eyes were hard and cold as January ice, and that image was strengthened by the white hair that sprayed

126

from beneath the old man's hat like wisps of snow drifting ahead of Montana winds.

Jasper was standing deferentially beside the newcomer, and he didn't meet Mordecai's eyes as the preacher approached.

When the old man spoke, his voice was low, taut, and his eyes poked into Mordecai like a stiletto.

"Helluva job you did on my boy, here," he hissed. "I'd like to know who the hell you think you are."

"Mordecai," the preacher said, offering his hand.

The old man's eyelids closed into slits.

"You don't know who I am, do you?"

The preacher shook his head.

"Newcombe. Dirk Newcombe. But you can call me mister."

"All right, mister."

The old man's eyes slitted again, and he growled through clenched teeth, "You aren't planning to take your belt off and whip me, are you, preacher?"

"Not unless you pull that knife out of your boot," Mordecai answered.

The two men glared at each other for a moment, and then Newcombe continued.

"You haven't answered my question: What in hell gives you the right to carve up one of my boys?"

"He was standing on the other end of a skinning knife," Mordecai said. "I was not in the mood to get skinned."

"He is my employee. He was trying to get you off my land — Bar O land. That's bar zero: bar nothing, preacher. Jasper had every right to use that knife."

"And I had every right to defend myself."

"Preacher," the old man said, sneering, "you are sorely trying my patience. Jasper told me about the Indian boy. I've told him before that I don't want any of them beggars around the slaughterhouse. They'll steal you blind if you give them half a chance.

"He understands that now," the old man continued, glaring at Jasper. "Now you understand something. I don't want you or any of those ki-yis at that plant. Just to make sure that they stay away, I've ordered Jasper to burn all the liver and hearts and kidneys we don't have orders for. I will no longer feed those beggars."

"Jasper was selling the meat to them."

The old man's temper flared. "Preacher, you don't listen good. I don't want those Indians at that plant. I don't want those Indians anywhere. That's all of it, I don't want to hear any more."

Newcombe paused, then his voice dropped a notch, and his eyes burned holes in

128

Mordecai. "There was a time when you could respect those people. They did what they had to do, just like I did. But their scat aren't men. They're beggars and drunks and thieves. Men like me killed the last good Indians. We should have killed them all."

And now the preacher's eyes bored into Newcombe's. "You'd think after all these years that you would have had enough of killing them."

The old man's voice rose a notch, and heads turned at the bar as the crowd strained to hear the words exchanged between Newcombe and this strange preacher.

"They're killing themselves. If they weren't so damn lazy, they could get work like everyone else. Only reason they starve is because they won't work."

"On your place?" the preacher asked. "Can they get work on your ranch or at your slaughterhouse or at any of the businesses around here that you own pieces of? Where are they going to work, Newcombe?"

The old man picked up a shot glass from the bar and slugged down his drink. "I heard you came into town on the train. That's a good way to leave."

Then he turned to Johnson. "Ben, you ought to be a little more careful about your customers. Businessman with friends like yours might be considered risky. Could be he'd have his loan pulled at the bank."

Jasper, two drinks under his belt, paused before following Newcombe to the door. "One day, preacher, we'll finish what you started."

"I always like to finish what I start, Jasper. I try really hard to do that."

The Cree and Chippewa and Métis people of the little village ringed the five-acre garden plot, motionless as posts. They were all watching Jack Ten Horses plow the land with two horses and equipment the preacher had rented for the day from a homesteader two miles downstream on the Milk.

Ten Horses was new to the task, and after the first straight line the preacher had cut into the earth at the edge of the field, the others waggled a bit, straightening as the neophyte gained experience.

The soil was dark and rich, moist still from winter snows and frost. The plow cut cleanly into the mix of sand and clay and silt, shuddering only occasionally from the resistance of a buried stone. Then one of the people lining the field would dart forward, dig out the stone, and carry it to a growing pile on the side of the field.

Ten Horses wasn't accustomed to the work

or the rough footing, and he reeled behind the plow. But he had too much pride to turn the work over to someone else, so he staggered along, stopping at each turn to take several deep breaths and to wipe his face with his shirttails.

The preacher and Judd huddled by the rock pile, talking softly in the warm spring sun. It was too early to plant, but the virgin ground needed to be broken and readied for the second week of May, when the long rows would be put into place.

And seeds had to be planted in the people, too, to ready them.

The smell of burning flesh came to them early that afternoon. Judd sensed it first and his nose pulled his eyes into the wind and the column of black smoke curling into the air from the slaughterhouse.

A fire built of cottonwood and kerosene, burning red and black against a sky too blue to be real, sputtered and crackled beside the slaughterhouse. Even from that distance, Judd could see heat waves rising from the blaze, distorting the pure, clean air of a Montana spring.

And as Judd watched, men — just black shapes against that bright blue sky — approached the fire with pitchforks writhing with guts and handfuls of hearts and kidneys and livers and pitched them on the inferno, watching while the flames licked at the meat.

One by one, the people at the garden had their attention pulled up the hill by the scent of burning meat.

Mordecai sighed, and pushed himself to his feet.

"Get some of the other kids to help gather wood, decent-sized so it will burn down to coals. Set others to building a fire pit as far across as you are tall and waist deep, here," he said, pointing to a swale in the shade of a cottonwood.

"Ask Mr. Old Hawk if he has a steel bar or a pipe about half again as tall as you are and some wire — not rusty. And bring your grandmother back with you.

"Please," the preacher said with a grin, and Judd grinned back, springing to the tasks the preacher had set him.

Mordecai walked up the hill toward the slaughterhouse, losing detail and color to the spring sky as he neared the top.

Judd watched the knot of men step out to meet the preacher, Jasper's arms punctuating words too far away to hear. Then some men stepped between the preacher and Jasper.

A moment later, the preacher reached into his pocket, money changed hands, and two of the men hauled a front quarter from the building and helped the preacher set it on his shoulder. The preacher staggered down the hill toward the people, bearing the makings of a feast.

The garden lay open, plowed, harrowed, and cleared of stones, the soil fine and fertile. All the people of the village had contributed to the effort, and now they sat in little knots around the fire pit, sharing talk and meat.

The air was redolent of roasting beef, and occasionally one or another of the people would pull himself to his feet, groaning theatrically, and step grinning to the fire for still another helping.

The sun was flirting with the horizon and it was a quiet time for the land and the people. Even the children's play had quieted, one after another pulling into his family's circle, seeking a mother's lap or a father's hand.

Judd hadn't seen Old Hawk and several of the other men leave or return, but they were sitting silently now, ringed around ancient, almost forgotten ceremonial drums.

The song began spontaneously, the men obeying instinct and not social order. The singers' voices melded into one, melded into the wail of centuries of prairie winds and the call of coyotes and the wonder of life and land.

The first beat of the drum drilled into Judd, seeking the core of his being.

He could see the singers across the fire, their faces flickering with flame and shadow as the sun slipped behind the horizon. He could see their hands moving, sticks slapping against the stretched hides of the drums. But now they were playing the nerves and muscles and sinews of the people around the fire, and the people were jerked into a shuffling dance, legs and bodies and minds compelled to find the old steps to match that ancient music.

Judd found himself in a circle of dancers, knees flexed and back bent to be nearer the earth, closer to the echo of those drums beating through rock and soil and earth and straight into his soul.

And as he danced, Judd lost his sense of self, became one with the people and the earth. Only vaguely did he realize that the preacher was dancing beside him, only vaguely did he see the sun rise the next morning and earth rushing up to meet his falling body.

The sun stabbing into Judd's eyes awakened him, and the pain when he twisted to free himself from its glare brought him into full consciousness. He ached from the bottom of his feet to the top of his head, and he groaned as he rolled over on his belly and pushed himself to his hands and knees. He shook his head, and a sharp pain stabbed him in the nape of the neck.

More carefully, now, he raised his head. There were bodies strewn still around the fire pit, some stirring, but most unmoving. The beef quarter, reduced to bones, hung still from the steel pipe over a bed of ashes, and on a pile of stones next to the pit sat his grandmother, eyes intent on the hill overlooking the garden site.

Judd's eyes followed hers to the hillside.

The preacher was standing on the hill, his arms raised as though to embrace God, and he was praying.

"Aieee," his grandmother crooned, and then she was silent, hiding her thoughts behind her clouded eyes.

Eight

Starlight pattered against the stained-glass windows of the church and died, leaving the Reverend Eli Timpkins in darkness.

The Reverend, back straight as the word of God, sat on the hard oak pews imported from Missouri — Montana wood was too soft to command the parishioners' attention on long Sunday meetings.

The windows — gray, black, and ghostly in the soft light — shrouded the kneeling man, attendants in a ritual Timpkins had observed since he had learned as a child that wonderful and terrible secret.

"Almighty Father," he whispered, the words lost in shadow. "Once again I am being tested by Satan. Your black angel follows me wherever I go, hoping that I will abandon you. He comes now in the guise of a preacher, but I see the wickedness of his heart.

"He would turn the people of Sanctuary against me and my work as he has in all those other towns, spreading dissension and evil over the earth. I cannot allow that again.

My time is too limited in this place of your creation."

Timpkins sighed. He tried to focus on his conversation with God, but the devil interfered, drawing his thoughts back to those other towns.

Reflexively his hand dropped to his ankle and he rubbed the scar tissue there. Always the scar itched when his mind pulled him back through the years to that little town in Nebraska.

He could still feel the heat from the bonfire and smell the mix of horses and sweat and hate. But even heavier on the air was the redolence of tar bubbling in a pot over the fire and the awful smell of chicken feathers.

Torches carried by the men cast the scene in an unreal, flickering light, and the sound of their voices was low and subdued, like the sound of a prairie wind, mild still, but carrying portent of storm. Bits and pieces poked out of the babble now and then like ice picks. *Castrate the bastard! Leave him hanging! Son-of-a-bitch!*

The Reverend had screamed when that hot tar first touched his body, screamed again as the feathers were matted into the mix. But even worse was that awful trip down the main street of town with men, women, and children lining the boardwalk on either side.

They threw curses at him like stones, and he grunted each time one found its mark. He had tried then to drive the words and the pain and the night from his mind, to focus on Golgotha, the place of the skull, and that day two millennia ago when Christ was nailed to the cross, when in his pain and suffering He cried out, "My God, my God, why has Thou forsaken me."

The Reverend had tried to say those same words, to hurl them back at the crowd, but only a pathetic mewl rose in his throat like bile.

And now in this dark church in Sanctuary, Montana, the Reverend mewled again, the sound breaking into shards against accusing windows.

The Reverend could feel Satan's strength. It lay over Sanctuary like a dark cloud, scattering his thoughts, making them dance like fall leaves in the breeze.

He *must* regain control! If he didn't, Satan would tell his lies with his serpent tongue, and the people would believe him and drive the Reverend out.

And then, just when Eli thought all was lost, he could feel God's strength flooding into him. The time for the final confrontation with the devil was near. The time of judgment was upon the land. The Reverend Eli

Timpkins could feel that, feel it in his bones, in his soul.

He stood then, steadying himself against the back of one of the pews, waiting for the blood to return to his cramped legs. He must be strong as he had been strong earlier that night during his meeting with the congregation's young people.

Even now the thought of that meeting brought a film of sweat to his forehead. He had stood silent before them, his eyes scourging them. They wanted his approval. They wanted him to smile at them, to tell them that they were no worse than anyone else. They wanted to be weak.

But he said nothing, speaking only with his eyes, letting his accusing gaze burn through the children's deceitful facade to the corruption beneath. They fidgeted in the pews under his glare, and when they could no longer meet his eyes, he had whispered so softly they strained to hear him. He courted their attention as carefully as a shopkeeper courts a customer, his voice building until it roared like the flames of a fire gone wild, consuming everything in its path.

The Spirit had raged within him as he told the children they were evil, hateful creatures and an abomination in the eyes of the Lord.

Sin would drip from their burning bodies in hell as the fat drips from a steak frying in the pan, he shouted. They would know pain as they had never known pain.

The younger children had cried then, frightened beyond caring what the other children thought. They sat wide-eyed in the pews, tears running in sheets down their faces.

A shudder ran through Timpkins' body as he remembered the terror on their faces, and an involuntary moan escaped his lips.

He had felt the power then, felt it deep in his gut, deep in his loins. His eyes roved through the ranks of children, feeding on their fear until the power cracked in him like a whip. And then his gaze reached Naomi Parkman.

Naomi's eyes met his. Her head was thrown back, mouth open and face flushed. Her arms were folded tightly across her sixteen-year-old body, and she squirmed ever so gently in her pew.

Naomi felt the power, too: she had since that first time when she was twelve and still tentative, and he had taught her what it meant to serve the Lord.

Naomi needed ministering to, and the Reverend called the class to a close. The children filed wide-eyed into the night, watching for the demons the Reverend had said were lurking at each corner, lusting for their souls. The younger children were still sobbing, holding hands with older brothers and sisters, souls hanging on the strength of their grip.

Benjamin asked Naomi to stay, and she smiled that knowing smile. And after the other children had gone, and the church was dark, he had blessed her with his body.

In each of the congregations the Reverend had served, one special child had emerged, one child who understood the power and the role that the Reverend was destined to play in the world.

But when those children's bellies began to swell with the wonderful secret the Reverend had planted there, the families of the congregations hadn't understood how special that gift was. They had turned on him, deaf ears not hearing the word, forcing him to flee for his life.

But now he was in Sanctuary, and he would run no farther. He would reveal the preacher Mordecai's real identity, and the battle between good and evil would be fought on the Montana prairie. The Reverend's army was stronger this time. He had instilled in his congregation the discipline necessary to fight the forces of evil.

And Mordecai — Satan incarnate — was forced to rely on sinners — pagans, men of strong drink like Doc Benjamin and blasphemers like Mary Dickens.

The Reverend would win this time. A tremor ran through Timpkins' body with the thought. He would stand before them, their faces upturned toward him and the fear of God in their eyes. And the Reverend Eli Timpkins would assume his rightful place, once and for all.

Nine

The spring sun lay on the land like a benediction, and Mary Dickens reveled in it. She was sitting on a pile of river rock, a lectern old as earth and new as the promise of the garden for the people laboring there.

Peas and radishes had been planted the first week of May, the people following cotton string and the preacher's directions across the tilled soil to leave straight, green rows.

The youngest of the village children were grazing through the peas, now, like deer browsing through a river bottom. Most of the peas had been picked and canned, steam rising from boiling water on cool spring mornings. The jars were stored in village shacks and for the first time in most of the villagers' lives, they had food set aside for the future. They took great pride in that.

The garden had become the focal point of the village; the people pulled away from the dump to weed or to watch the children, or simply to bask in a common sense of proprietorship.

And now the older children were perched

around Mary, picking through coverless primers too worn for the school on the hill, treasures for children who had never touched, or been touched by, books.

The school had been underway since the close of the regular session, and Mary loved the time she spent with these quiet people. As she had expected, Judd was bright, picking up the rudiments of reading and arithmetic almost too easily. He had become the unofficial "second teacher" of the outdoor school, helping the children translate Cree thoughts into English and English into the written word.

Judd's grandmother had abandoned her rocker in favor of a stump near the river rocks school. She sat there in the early-morning hours, cloudy eyes watching the children of the village learn the white man's scratching, watching her grandson pull words from the primer's pages and thoughts from the other children. For the first time in Judd's memory, he could see the hint of a smile flit occasionally across her face as the shadow of a cloud skips across the prairie in summer.

Judd and the preacher had built sturdy pens of chicken wire and rough-cut lumber to house the rabbits and chickens the preacher seemed to have plucked from thin air.

And as the peas lost their pods and the

radishes their roots, the people cut the plants and fed them to the rabbits, taking care to leave the peas' nitrogen-rich roots in the ground.

Chicken eggs, warmed by the stove and lying like seeds on a blanket, incubated in the Old Hawk home, children stopping each day to turn them and to listen for the pecking of chicks trying to free themselves from the shells.

Jack Ten Horses had stopped his nightly trips to the alleys behind Sanctuary bars; instead he plunged into the management of the garden, directing others where to weed and where to till.

Ten Horses and the preacher had engineered a ditch to carry water to the garden from a small creek that ran just west of the dump, and he and some of the other men had spent the past week bent over shovels and picks, carving the ditch from the sandy soil of the river bottom.

Ten Horses had become one with the people again, and for the first time in his adult life he felt that he was doing something worthy of a man. Connie Old Hawk's appendectomy had cured him of the rancor he felt toward the villagers, and the villagers turned to him for leadership as naturally as their ancestors had turned to his great-grandfather in times long past.

He was leaner now, and long-muscled, the hard work having stripped away the ashes of long nights spent in the company of a bottle of whiskey and bad deeds.

Doc made weekly trips to the village, leaving with a renewed spring to his step and a dozen eggs or a fresh rabbit in return for his care.

And as the people of the village pulled together in the magic of that warm Montana spring, the preacher pulled gradually away. More and more he deferred questions to Ten Horses and to Judd. More and more he sat by himself on the hill where Judd had seen him praying that morning after the dance, shedding his coat as though to absorb the sun, the time, the land, and the people through the pores of his skin.

Still, even on mornings like this when it seemed that the earth was lit with nothing less than the warmth of God's smile, Judd's mind skipped from the book in his lap to a cloud of thick oily smoke boiling from burning flesh at the slaughterhouse. It hung over the village like a portent.

His mind bounced back to it with a persistence that worried him, and the wind whispered across the nape of his neck like an omen as he helped his grandmother back to their shack.

The clamber of hooves across the step outside jerked Judd into full consciousness. He had been lying in a half sleep — that time when the subconscious and the conscious meet — not certain if the sound of cows bawling outside was real or imagined.

From the first time he stepped up that hill to the slaughterhouse and the abuse Jasper and the others heaped upon him, Judd had dreamed of cattle. But they didn't bawl as the cattle were bawling outside, because the cattle in his dreams had no tongues — or hides or guts or legs. They stood stripped in pens, watching Jasper and his knife, waiting for Judd to trade a quarter for their hearts and livers, watching him with wonder in their eyes as he carried bits and pieces of them downhill to the people.

The door rattled. Dream cattle didn't bump into doors. But what were cattle doing in the village? He could hear, too, the whistle and whoop of drovers.

Judd climbed from beneath his covers. His grandmother was already at the door, peering outside through the single pane of cracked glass. But her eyes were too cloudy to put anything but vague shapes to the sounds, black against black.

Judd fumbled around the table for matches.

He lit one and touched the flame to the wick of an old brass railroad lantern he had found bent and discarded by the track. A globe of yellow light limped into the room. Judd carried the light to the door and tried to step outside, but a passing steer brushed him back into the shack. He stood there, peering through the feeble light at a scene he didn't comprehend.

A river of bellowing, horn-clicking cattle was flowing through the little village. The herd was tightly packed, and occasionally an animal bumped into a shack or stumbled against something left lying on the ground, but the missteps were nothing more than ripples in a stream. The animals moved on as relentlessly as the Milk in flood.

And on the outside of the herd, Judd could hear men on horseback. Some spoke in whispers to the cattle, as though they were divulging secrets to a friend; others yelled "yip, yip, yip" and spurred their horses as they cut off animals attempting to escape the crush flowing through the village.

All were intent on moving the animals and nothing else. They seemed oblivious to the dark faces painted in shadow, soft light, and fear, that were framed against open doors. They seemed oblivious, impervious, inhuman — dark messengers from dark places bent on a task too evil for mortals to comprehend.

The people in the village shrank back into the shadows, too horrified to close their doors to the scene outside, too frightened to call out, to draw the attention of these dark strangers.

And still the cattle moved past until suddenly they were gone, disappearing up the hill toward the slaughterhouse, the only sign of their passing faint sounds from the hill and dust hanging in the early-morning air.

The people stepped out into silence, stumbling as their feet reached ground torn by the passing of hundreds of hooves. They stood there until the message passed from their feet to their minds.

Judd murmured "the garden," and a wave of keening, lonesome and cold as a winter gale, swept through the group. The lights bobbed away from the village then, backtracking the cattle until they seemed faint stars lying low on the horizon, winking against the predawn blackness, blackest time of all.

* Judd sneaked up the back stairs of the hotel, flinching whenever a step protested under his weight. If he were caught, he would be branded thief and thrown in jail. But he had no choice, so he inched up the stairs and down the hallway, every nerve tingling, every sense

singing warnings. When he rapped at the door, the sound seemed to boom through the building.

"Preacher," he whispered. "Preacher, please open the door."

Judd heard the scuff of a chair inside and a moment later, the door opened. The preacher was fully dressed and shaved, even though it was still dark outside, minutes yet before false dawn.

Judd spoke in a rush. "Jack Ten Horses has been hurt bad, real bad. He tried to stop some men from driving cattle though the garden, and they ran the cattle over him, too.

"It's all gone. All of it, and Jack, he's — I think he's going to die. He's hurt something awful, preacher."

"Get Doc. I reserved a wagon for early this morning. Take him down to the camp, and I'll meet you there with the wagon."

Judd nodded and sprang for the door. He paused there for a moment, waiting for the preacher. "Why did you rent the wagon?"

"Thought we might need it today at the garden. Guess I was right."

Judd nodded, but he was looking at the preacher from the corner of his eyes as they hurried down the hall to Doc's room.

Dawn had just cracked the eastern horizon

150

as Judd and Doc rushed down the hill toward the village. Neither had spoken on the walk from the hotel, each occupied with his own thoughts. They could see the people now, gathered around what appeared to be a pile of clothing dumped and forgotten on the northern edge of the garden.

Doc's breath left him in one long sigh, and a plume of vapor chased it into the chilly morning air. As they neared the group, it parted. Ten Horses, or what was left of him, lay in a heap at the end of the passage, and Doc knelt beside the stricken man.

Ten Horses was a mass of injuries. It seemed that every steer passing through the village that morning had stepped on him. Deep, ugly bruises and cuts marked his skin and thin trickles of blood ran unabated from his nose and the corner of his mouth. His left arm lay at an odd angle, and Doc knew it was broken. A bent right leg and labored breathing indicated more broken bones.

But Doc was worried most about what else those hooves might have done to Ten Horses. The young man appeared to be cold, in shock undoubtedly, and a ruptured spleen or kidney or liver might be hemorrhaging into the abdominal cavity. Too, one of the hooves might have struck deep into his chest and bruised his heart.

Doc sighed and leaned back from his preliminary examination just in time to hear the clop of hooves and the rattle and creak of a wagon as the preacher pulled up.

Doc looked up and shook his head, and the preacher climbed down.

The preacher knelt beside Ten Horses and took his head in his hands. Ten Horses' eyes opened, and a murmur ran through the crowd. His voice was little more than a whisper.

"Cattle in garden . . . tried to stop them . . . Jasper ran over me with his horse. All I remember."

"You sure it was Jasper?" Mordecai asked.

"I could hear him laugh. I will never forget his laughter. Even now, I hear it in my dreams." His eyes closed then, and his head slipped to one side.

One of the women in the crowd began to keen, the sound cutting through the morning like ice crystals borne on a north wind, but the preacher held up his hand.

"He's not dead," he said in Cree, looking around the group, his eyes settling on Judd. "Spread those blankets in the back of the wagon.

"And you," he added, pointing at the three nearest men. "You all help me load him. We must be very, very careful. He is near to death. You'll have to come with Doc and me to the surgery to help us carry him inside.

"Judd, you go get Sheriff Timothy. Tell him to meet us at the surgery. Tell him he doesn't have time for his morning cup of coffee."

The crowd broke apart as the men fled to their tasks.

Sheriff Timothy scuttled sideways, crab-like, through the door of the surgery, a habit he had acquired to accommodate the width and bulk of his shoulders. He was short and squat, built like a block with no break in the line between his chest and hips. His face was round as a full moon and underlined with a chin that could split granite. When he spoke, his voice rolled out like the rumble of thunder.

"The boy," he said, his neck inclining stiffly toward Judd, "says you had some trouble."

"Jack had some trouble," the preacher replied, nodding at the table.

"Jack *is* trouble," Timothy said, with no hint of a smile.

The sheriff walked over to the table and watched Doc strip off Ten Horses' clothing, his fingers probing the extent of the man's injuries.

Timothy shook his head. "Holy Mother of Mary. Somebody did one hell of a job on him. Can't say even *he* had that coming."

"They walked a herd of cattle over him. Can't say anyone has that coming to him," the preacher growled, his voice dropping to meet the sheriff's.

Doc was talking, now, describing Ten Horses' injuries to set them straight in his mind. "Left arm broken, both the radius and the ulna. Almost at right angles. Have to set that right away, and the left leg. Lucky there. It's the fibula, and that won't lay him up so long."

Doc stepped back from the table, straightening and stretching his back. He turned to look at the preacher. "The bones will heal. Should have full use of them, at least until arthritis settles in, but there's nothing we can do about that. The bruises will heal, too.

"But Jesus, this man must be in pain!"

Doc rubbed his face in his hands, cupping his chin in his palms.

"I can take care of the bones, and maybe I can do something for the pain, although I have to be careful there. Wouldn't take much to stop his breathing.

"But this!" Doc's hands ranged over the upper left quadrant of Ten Horses' belly. The skin was stretched tight and rigid.

"His spleen is ruptured. No question about that. Could be, too, that he has head injuries.

"Nothing I can do about either of those injuries, not yet anyway. So the best thing to do is to set the arm and leg and give him a quarter grain of morphine for the pain and hope the spleen stops bleeding on its own. Sometimes it does, and sometimes it doesn't.

"Judd, maybe you wouldn't mind giving me a hand with this, and give the preacher a chance to talk to the sheriff."

Judd nodded, and the preacher and the sheriff stepped into the waiting room, settling into a couch that lined one wall.

"He tell you what happened?"

The preacher nodded. "Early morning, before first light, some yahoos brought a herd of cattle up through the river bottom and across a garden Jack has been working on."

"Ten Horses has been gardening?"

"Doing a good job of it, too. Anyway, he tried to head off the cattle, and one of the drovers — a man named Jasper Higgins — ran him down. Ten Horses was knocked unconscious and the herd was driven over him."

The sheriff was silent for a moment, his mind picking methodically through the web of the story looking for frayed edges.

"If it was full dark, how could Ten Horses

know it was Jasper?"

"He recognized him by his laugh."

"By his laugh? Charley Altheimer, Esquire, would have fun with that," Timothy spat. "He represents all the Bar Nothing boys. Dirk Newcombe would hang Charley on Ten Horses' neck like a noose, and you can bet by the time he finished, a jury would be ready to finish the job."

"Are you saying you won't do anything?"

Timothy's voice took on an edge like a rock crusher with a granite boulder stuck in its craw.

"Didn't say that at all. You want me to, I'll arrest Jasper. What I'm telling you is that it'll be Jasper's word against Jack's, and Altheimer will twist that jury around his finger and shove it up Jack's . . . rear end.

"What'll it be, preacher?"

"It won't be justice," the preacher said. "Whatever it is, it won't be justice."

Doc was still hovering over Jack Ten Horses when Judd and the preacher opened the door to the surgery. Doc glanced up, distracted for a moment, and waved his hand before returning his attention to his patient.

"Jack will be all right," the preacher said as they stepped through the door. "Doc will make sure of that."

Outside, the three men from the village were waiting in the wagon box. The preacher and Judd climbed into the seat, and the preacher slapped the reins on the horse's back.

"We'll take the men back to the village, and then return the wagon to the livery."

"I thought you had hired the wagon for work in the garden."

"What?" the preacher asked, obviously distracted. "Oh, I did. Not much we can do there now, though, with a wagon."

"What were you going to use it for?"

"Some chores needed doing. That's all."

The wagon rattled along for nearly a quarter of a mile before Judd could ask the question that had been plaguing him all morning. "You knew Jack was going to be hurt, didn't you?"

Mordecai cupped his chin in his hand and turned his full attention to Judd. "How could I know that?"

Judd shrugged, but not once on the long trip back to the village did his eyes leave the preacher's face.

Ten

The night was pitch black, and the preacher, riding more by ear than eye, nudged his horse along on the prairie above the Milk.

He stopped, silencing the squeak of leather and the jangle of the bridle, to listen. A coyote caught in the mystery of the night barked somewhere ahead, and a prairie breeze popped in the preacher's ears, but silence heavy and black underlined those faint sounds.

Mordecai knew steers grazed the pasture, but it sprawled across twenty square miles, and the animals could be anywhere. He swung his offside leg across the saddle horn, turning his attention to the black sky while the horse reached down to tug at the tender spring grass. The moon would be up before long, painting the prairie silver and black, and Mordecai wanted to be clear of the Bar Nothing before then.

There! The rattle and thump of creatures running, hooves striking the ground. Cattle? No, these animals were bouncing, not running — mule deer disturbed while they nibbled at sage redolent in the cool night air. The deer would have hidden in the blackness until he passed, but when he stopped their nerve broke, and they ran.

The coulee creased the prairie near here. Cattle had worn a path down its walls to a tiny creek and reservoir below, seeking water and soft grass in the day and beds at night to escape the wind skipping across the prairie.

The preacher looked up, his eyes roving the skies for the Big and Little Dippers. They were just where they should be — over his left shoulder — so he was still traveling east. Any time now.

Mordecai's dead reckoning proved remarkably accurate. The gelding ambled along for less than a hundred yards before coming to an abrupt halt. The preacher, having had no warning of the animal's intent, lurched forward in the saddle. He waited in blackness so still, he could hear his own heartbeat and the rustle of the wind through the grass. What had the horse sensed ahead in that void?

But the night was empty, and the preacher touched his heels to the gelding's flanks. The horse stepped ahead and off the edge of a hill Mordecai couldn't see, clumping stiff-legged down the steep wall of the coulee.

The preacher leaned into the stirrups. Shale poked black and slick as oil from the coulee walls, promising a dangerous tumble for an unwary rider. But the hillside here was clothed in grass, and the horse bottomed out without slipping.

Mordecai heard one steer ambling away. The animals weren't unduly spooky. That would make his job a lot easier. The steep coulee walls would be as good as fifty riders funneling the cattle toward the Milk.

Mordecai would cut ten head from the herd down there, drop the barbed-wire fence and drive them across the Milk and into the heavy brush along the river and then go back and fix the fence. It could be days before a cowboy stumbled on the trail, and even then he might pass without investigating. It could be that Dirk Newcombe would never know he was missing the cattle.

The preacher touched his heels to the gelding, humming "Rock of Ages" as he pushed the cattle down the coulee.

A curl of rancid smoke rose into the still air from a fire set the night before at the dump. But that was the only movement on the river bottom.

The garden, fenced now, stood abandoned, green lines marking the emergence of new plants, and the school stood like a sentinel guarding one corner of it.

After Jack Ten Horses was almost killed, the people abandoned the garden, but the preacher had promised them meat if they would reseed the parcel, build a strong fence, and finish the ditch.

Once work began, the garden pulled the people together. They met there each day until the morning when the preacher announced they had earned their pay, and there was meat waiting on the bottom downriver.

The people had disappeared then, the children lingering for half a day at the school, their minds and their eyes pulled downstream until finally Mary Dickens had waved them away. They disappeared like smoke.

Mary sighed. She might as well go back to the teacherage. Still, she had been curious about the killing place, as the people called it, and a moment later she followed her curiosity and the path down the riverbank, enjoying the shade cast by the cottonwoods and the heavy smell of mint.

She didn't hurry, stopping to pick the wild roses that grew along the river bottom and then to pick the fine, sharp thorns from her fingers. She cupped her hands around the fragile pink blossoms, immersed in their delicate beauty and subtle scent.

She smelled the camp before she saw it, wood smoke curling through the river bottom. The smoke grew heavier, seasoned with the odor of curing meat as she neared.

And when Mary Dickens stepped into the killing place, she felt as though she had stepped through a rip in time.

Willows from the riverbank had been cut and woven into racks. They hung heavy with meat over slow-burning smoky fires, tended by women with faces so dark it appeared that they were curing, too.

One fire, coals red in the dim light, sputtered as it licked at grease dripping from a side of beef turning slowly under the ministrations of a woman Mary didn't know.

The men lay in little knots on the grass, talking and smoking, their laughter and the squeals of children competing with the murmur of the Milk.

Trees at the other edge of the clearing were hid in smoke, dark and obscure. Sunlight streamed through the cottonwoods overhead like the shafts of arrows loosed by the sun. But that light cast no shadows, not in the dark, intoxicating smoke.

A shudder teased the hair on the nape of Mary's neck. There was something primitive here, something dark hidden in the smoke and the people's skin and in their eyes. She remembered that day last fall . . .

Mary had packed a picnic lunch to walk

162

the river bottom.

Now she followed game trails upstream along the Milk, avoiding patches of impenetrable wild rose and willow.

At one point, the Milk looped to the east, opening a large clearing below the bluff that defined the ancient course of the river. She heard voices and made her way through the trees to the clearing.

Three men toiled there, dragging bones from below the bluff and dumping them into a wagon. They stopped occasionally to wipe the sweat from their foreheads, but the breaks lasted only seconds before they dug into the hillside again.

Mary watched until the scent of old wood smoke and leather pulled her eyes back toward the river. She started when she saw an old man standing only a step away.

He was dressed in wool pants and a red flannel shirt worn soft and brown through the years. Over the shirt was a leather vest adorned with elk teeth, and on his feet were moccasins laced halfway up his calves.

The old man's hair was white, thin and wispy, spraying from beneath a flat-brimmed, high-crowned black hat. A feather poked like an afterthought from the hat's brim.

Skin, dry and crinkled as parchment, stretched over the sharp, protruding bones of his face. Only his nose seemed to have any weight to it. Fat as a camel's hump, it dominated his face, overwhelming tiny black eyes that twinkled in its shadow like stars on a dark night.

"Aieee," he said, his eyes wandering past Mary to the men working on the hillside. "Is it not a mystery?"

Mary took a step back. "Where did you come from?"

The old man pondered the question for a moment. "I have been following them," he said, his finger settling on the wagon. "Is it not a mystery?"

"I mean just now. Where did you come from just now? I didn't hear you."

The old man waved his arm behind him. "Back there. Indians move without making noise. Didn't you know that?" His eyes probed her face. "Don't you read those dime novels? All Indians move without making noise."

His shoulders shook as he laughed at his own joke, but then his eyes moved back to the working men and the laughter stopped. "Aieee, is it not a mystery?"

"What is this place?" Mary asked.

"Pishkin."

"Pishkin?"

"Yes."

"What is pishkin?" Mary asked, exasperation creeping into her voice.

"Come sit beside my fire," the old man said. "I will tell you about the pishkin, and maybe you can tell me about the mystery."

Mary hesitated. She didn't know the old man. His dress and background and speech put him outside her frame of reference. She didn't know what niche, if any, he fit in, and she found that frightening. But her curiosity proved stronger than her wariness, and she followed the old man deeper into the trees, listening carefully to see if he could, indeed, walk without making any noise.

The fire burned dirty orange and quiet on cottonwood branches and leaves. The old man had built it in front of a fallen cottonwood, and he settled on that log after feeding the fire from a pile of wood nearby.

He gestured for Mary to sit beside him and began rummaging through a small bag he carried on a thong over his shoulder. A moment later, he pulled a pipe from the bundle and a package of tobacco. He packed the pipe, lit it with a stick from the fire and then turned his attention to Mary.

"Pishkin is Blackfoot for buffalo jump," he said. "I am a Blackfoot. In the old days, before even the horse, my people drove buffalo over that bluff back there.

"Then we would camp along the river. The men would smoke and talk while the women smoked and dried the meat and made pemmican and cured robes. It was a good time. We always had plenty to eat, and the children would hunt rabbits and gophers and swim and do children's things.

"Pishkins were good, but bad too. Sometimes we killed more buffalo than we could eat, and they would rot unless our brothers the coyotes and wolves came to feed on them in the night. The manitou did not like us to waste the great gift the buffalo were.

"So when the horse came to my people, we stopped using pishkins. There was not so much waste in hunting the buffalo on horseback."

The old man stopped talking, and a grin crossed his face. "It might be, too, that we hunted on horseback because it was more fun.

"That pishkin" — his arm swept over his shoulder in the direction of the men and the wagon — "was used for many years. The bones of many buffalo lay there.

"But why do those men pick the bones and carry them away in wagons? This is the mystery. I have followed them now for the spring and the summer and the fall and still I do not know."

166

The old man's face was twisted into a question mark as he looked at Mary.

"They sell the bones for bonemeal," she said.

"Aieee. I have been told that, but do they eat this bonemeal?"

"No, but — "

"Or wear it to keep them warm in the winter? Or burn it in their fires?"

Mary shook her head again.

"Ah," he said. "That is what I thought."

The old man sat silently, watching the fire eat the cottonwood.

"You know what I think?" he said, not taking his eyes from the fire. "I think that those men are taking the buffalo bones so that no one will ever know about the buffalo."

He sighed, and Mary could feel the resignation in that breath of air.

"I think that the same men who sent the soldiers and the smallpox and wiped out the buffalo sent those men over there. I think these men were sent to wipe out the trail my people left on this land so that no one will know we were ever here.

"They must hate us so. If I follow these men, maybe they will lead me to the others and they can tell me what we have done to make them hate us."

The old man straightened on the log, his

head swiveling toward the pishkin. "They are leaving now. I must go so I can follow them.

"Aieee, is it not a great mystery?"

He rose then, smiled at Mary, and walked back toward the wagon, disappearing seconds later in the trees, just disappearing. . . .

Mary shuddered as she watched the women busy at their task of curing the meat. She felt that she was encroaching, that she didn't belong, that this time and space belonged to the people from the village.

' But deeper — below her Eastern upbringing, below her years in school, below her pale skin — she felt at home. She sat down on a rock, anchored with bonds as tenuous as the smoke from the fire and as strong as the sinews of her body.

It was then that she noticed the preacher, the sharp contrast between black coat and white shirt softened by the smoke in the clearing. His attention was focused across the river, and her eyes followed his up the hillside to a barbedwire fence.

Judd had crossed the river and backtracked cattle to the fence that separated the Bar Nothing ranch from the river bottom. He seemed intent on the posts, examining the points at which the nails had been pulled free to drop the fence, allowing for the passage of the cattle, and then nailed up again.

Judd turned and gazed across the river. Even at that distance, his body seemed stiff, wary. His eyes met the preacher's and they stared across that gulf. They were still staring when Mary looked away.

Eleven

Sheriff Timothy rolled off the slaughterhouse hill toward the Indian shacks like a boulder, and faces hard as stone hid behind cracked windows to watch him come.

Children, jerked into shacks by older brothers and sisters, read their parents' faces and retreated into corners and under beds and huddled there in silence.

There was only one reason the sheriff came to the little village by the dump: to haul one of the people to jail and maybe to prison.

Minds skipped over the past week, wondering for which sin they would be held accountable. Parents worried about the occasions their children had been out of sight. Had one of them broken a window or taken something from an alley behind a house or store? Maybe Sam Jenkins, who traded rotgut whiskey to the people, had told the sheriff. It was illegal for Montana Indians to have whiskey.

Shrouded in shadow, Judd leaned against the stove in his grandmother's shack. He watched the sheriff rumble into camp, and he imagined for a moment that the earth trembled beneath the lawman's feet. His grandmother had made herself invisible, melding into the contours of the rocking chair. Judd had not yet moved outside. Her dark face bled into the dark clothing she wore, and only her eyes — nearly opaque now with cataracts — hinted of the life in that pile of rags.

Judd braced himself, but still he started when he heard the word.

"Outside!" rattled through the village like the first stones in a summer hailstorm. Judd looked at his grandmother and stepped toward the door.

Throughout the village, doors scuffed open and men stepped through. Their faces framed by the windows in the shacks, women and children waited inside to see how their lives would be changed by this day.

"Somebody dropped a Bar Nothing fence, two, three miles downstream," the sheriff said. "Looks like he took ten or fifteen head across the Milk into the river bottom."

The sheriff doffed his hat, running his handkerchief around the sweatband and wiping his forehead before returning the white Stetson to his head.

"Cattle seem to have disappeared. No cattle. No hides. No guts. Nothing."

"But it looks like a lot of people got together across that creek" — his left hand rose to his face, and Timothy scratched his temple — "to cure some meat.

"Most everything is gone, but it's got that smell," he said, turning his face into the gentle breeze. "Just like here. You folks know anything about this?"

Silence. Absolute silence.

Another door opened and Jack Ten Horses, propped on a crutch, hobbled out on his step.

"This doesn't concern you, Jack. Doc says you were still in the surgery when we figure it happened."

"It concerns me," Ten Horses said.

Timothy's eyes roved through the camp and settled on Judd.

"Judd, you know anything about this?"

Judd met the sheriff's eyes, but he didn't speak.

"I know you speak English, Judd, so I'll ask you again. Do you know anything about this?"

Silence.

Timothy sighed.

"You people could have saved me a little time, and the judge might have taken that into consideration. But you'd best know that I'll get to the bottom of this. You can count on that.

"Dirk Newcombe is madder'n hell. He

put up a five-hundred-dollar reward for the arrest and conviction of the rustler."

Timothy rubbed the back of his neck. "Five hundred dollars is a lot of money. Sooner or later I'll get my man."

More silence.

The sheriff sighed again. "Any of you want to talk, you know where to find me."

He turned and rumbled toward the hill, and it seemed again that the earth trembled beneath his feet.

The people stayed in the village that day, leaving the garden to the grasshoppers and the hot June sun. Whenever children left the shacks, they were called back in hushed tones.

The preacher appeared around noon, walking down the hill with steps so light he seemed subject to the whim of the gentle wind dancing through the shacks.

When he reached the village, he pulled up a three-legged chair somebody had hauled from the dump, fished out his pocketknife from a trouser pocket, picked up a stick from the ground, and sat down.

The people stood in shadows behind dirty windows and watched the preacher whittle, like critics seeking meaning in an obscure theatrical performance.

The preacher's knife flashed, slicing light from the sun, yellow shavings drifting through the heavy air to a tiny pile at his feet. Flies buzzed through the air, and a meadowlark called from the edge of town.

Those were the only sounds until two doors scraped open and Judd and Jack Ten Horses stepped out. Neither acknowledged the other, but they met on the wide path that threaded its way through the village and stalked toward the preacher.

Mordecai continued whittling for several minutes after Judd and Ten Horses stepped in front of him. Then he folded his knife and slipped it into his pocket.

"I could hear the corn crying for water," the preacher said. "Came down to see why no one was irrigating."

"Timothy was here," Ten Horses said, and when the preacher didn't reply, he continued. "He wanted to know about some cattle — ten to fifteen head, he said — that had been rustled from the Bar Nothing, downriver from here.

"I'd guess it was ten head, wouldn't you, preacher?"

"I don't know anything about rustled cattle," Mordecai replied, rubbing his fingers over the stick, feeling for flaws left in the wood by the sharp blade of his knife.

"Helluva coincidence that Newcombe comes up short ten head the same time you

174

deliver ten head to the people."

"Sometimes things aren't as they seem."

"Sorry, preacher, but I don't believe in coincidences."

"What do you believe in?"

Ten Horses' voice dropped to a whisper. "For a while, preacher, I believed in you. I really thought you were different.

"But now I think that you rustled those cattle, and we'll be the ones to go to jail. Preacher, they'll kill me if they get me into jail again."

Mordecai shook his head.

"You shouldn't believe *in* people, Jack. Trust them, love them, but only believe in God."

Mordecai shifted his seat on the wobbly chair. "But you can believe me now, Jack. You won't go to jail."

"How the hell do you know that?" Ten Horses hissed. "You know what I think, preacher? I think you were in this from the beginning. I think Newcombe sent for you so you could make us think you were our friend, that you cared.

"I think he set it up for you to rustle those cattle so we'd get the blame. I've heard him. We're like a thorn in his side, and he had to get somebody we trusted to do his dirty work for him.

"And we believed you. That's the part that's so damn hard to take. After Connie and Doc and the teacher and the garden, I really believed in you.

"Then Judd told me about the wagon. How you had hired the wagon the morning Newcombe drove the cattle over . . . the garden. You knew what would happen, and only Newcombe could have told you.

"Preacher, if I wasn't so busted up, I'd kill you right now. So help me, I'd kill you right now."

The preacher stood and put his arms on Ten Horses' shoulders. Tears collecting in the man's eyes spilled over, and Ten Horses wept.

At first Mary Dickens thought she imagined the rapping. She had very few visitors during her time in Sanctuary and certainly none at this time in the morning. She rolled over to go back to sleep, but then she heard the rapping again, more insistent this time.

She climbed from bed, slipped her robe over her nightgown, and stepped cautiously to the bedroom door, opening it just enough to peer through the window in the front door.

Doc Benjamin had his face pressed against the windowpane. Now what in the world would he be doing out here at this time of day?

Mary stepped to the door and opened it

about as wide as the question on her face.

"Mary, I've got to talk to you. They've got the preacher in jail — "

"What?"

"In jail — for rustling!"

"Start a fire, Doc, while I get dressed. I'll put some coffee on so we can talk." Mary disappeared into the bedroom.

Doc tried to get his thoughts in order so he could explain the remarkable events that had transpired that morning.

Doc had been called out early to the surgery. Doctor Wilson had taken a week off to go fishing, the first vacation he'd had in years, and Doc was filling in.

There was nothing special about the call. Two cowboys had gotten into a fight in the Silver Dollar. One chewed off the other's ear, but the victim was too drunk to notice it was missing until he'd ridden nearly all the way to the Bar Nothing. By the time he returned to Sanctuary, the wound had clotted, and it was just a question of cleaning the stump and putting in the stitches.

The cowhand's stomach was churning, and when Doc mentioned that the only ill effect the young man was likely to suffer was that his hat would ride a little crooked, he stumbled out the door and vomited. He vomited again when one deputy offered to arrest the ear biter even though, he said, he was not anxious to tangle with a man who ate raw meat.

The wound was totally unremarkable, and the deputies gossiped as they watched Doc do his work. Doc overheard only bits and pieces of the conversation, but one line snapped into his consciousness.

"First time I've ever arrested a preacher," one deputy said. "Never would have taken him for a rustler."

The sheriff's office and jail was a little two-room brick building just a skip and a jump from the courthouse. Steel bars glinted from each of the windows in the morning light, and a red geranium sat in the window of the sheriff's office.

When Mary and Doc stepped through the door, Timothy was dumping the residue from a two-day-old pot of coffee on the plant. He looked up, muttering, "If there were such a thing as rotgut coffee, Whimple would make it, but this geranium seems to like it."

Indeed, the geranium seemed to be flourishing, stretching out big, wide leaves to greet the early sun in the window. "Did you know that Whimple's running against me in the next election?" Timothy asked, raising an eyebrow so he could peek past a fleshy fold of skin at his two visitors. "He's down at the Silver Dollar now telling everybody how he'd run this office if he were sheriff. It would serve him right if he won — he could play sheriff, and I'd go down to the bar and politic. But I don't suppose you're down here to talk about that."

Doc shook his head.

"I can't figure it," Timothy said, rubbing his chin with the back of his hand. "Not much for religion myself, but if I was to go to a church, I'd go to the one he's squiring in the Silver Dollar.

"He's short on speeches and long on doing, and he doesn't seem to have the mean streak that . . . some do."

Timothy shook his head, and then continued. "I swear, if words were weapons, I'd be arresting the Reverend Eli twice a day for assault. But there's some that think that he preaches the only brand of religion worth worrying about. Takes all kinds, I guess."

Timothy straightened, peering one-eyed at Doc. "You aren't packing, are you, Doc?"

"Packing?"

"Guns? Knives? Whiskey?"

Doc shook his head.

"Ma'am?"

Mary's eyes flashed. "If you think I am the kind of woman who — "

"Don't think anything of the kind. Just that I let a nice young lady in to see a 'friend' of hers, one time in Nebraska. She shot him dead. I didn't think she was packing, either.

"So now I ask."

Mary's voice softened. "No, sheriff, I am not carrying any weapons or whiskey."

"Didn't think you were."

Timothy pulled a ring of keys off the wall and opened the heavy wooden door that separated his office from the jail. "'Bout the only thing this door does is keep me from having to listen to the drunks wrestle with their snakes. No offense, Doc."

Doc shook his head. No offense.

Mordecai was lying on a bunk in one of the three cells, head propped on his hands, eyes on the ceiling as though the secret of life were written there.

He turned as Mary, Doc, and the sheriff stopped in front of the cell.

"Might be you can get him to tell you what the hell is going on," Timothy said. "He won't tell me anything."

"Ask and ye shall receive," Mordecai said with a grin.

Timothy snorted. "Where you from?"

"Everywhere."

"Where'd you go to seminary?"

"Everywhere."

"Where were you before you came here?"

"Everywhere."

Timothy snorted again, and Mordecai laughed.

"You're pretty damned chipper for a man like as not will wind up in prison. You won't like prison, preacher, not one bit."

"I've been in prison before."

"You have?" Timothy asked. "Where?" and then he spotted Mordecai's grin. "Never mind, I know. Everywhere."

Mordecai nodded.

"Miss Dickens, Doc," Timothy said, tipping his hat. "I leave this rustler to you. Try to get him to talk. He isn't doing himself any good playing cute."

Mary waited until she heard the door to Timothy's office close behind her, and then she asked, "What's this all about?"

"They say I rustled some Bar Nothing beef."

"Did you?"

"Would a preacher rustle cattle?"

"You haven't answered my question."

"Let's put it this way. I did what I did for a reason. I don't want to talk right now about what I did or why I did it."

"Are you going to plead guilty?"

"And throw myself on the mercy of the court? I've found little mercy around here.

No, Doc, I want a jury trial."

Mordecai walked to the bars, reaching out to touch Mary's and Doc's shoulders. He grinned then, and Doc felt as though he'd been touched by a warm summer breeze.

The preacher's grin softened and was replaced by concern. He said, "Judd's hiding across the street behind the haberdashery. I'd appreciate it if you were to ask him to come over here."

He waited then for Doc's nod.

"Walk soft, Doc. The boy's likely to run if he hears you coming."

Twelve

Judd sat across the table from his grandmother, watching dust motes dance in the
stream of light from the early-morning sun.

No words passed between the two, but they
were speaking one to the other, Judd pouring
out without words the anguish he felt and his
grandmother listening without hearing.

Judd spoke in the way he fidgeted in his
chair, in the tilt of his head and the sighs that
crashed through the stream of light, sending
the dust motes careering into darkness.

His grandmother listened only with her
eyes, her mind peeking past the cataracts at
this boy she had reared . . . her boy.

Even now, Grandmother felt her breath
catch when she thought about Judd's mother.
Grandmother's years were already long then,
and the baby entered the world with great
pain, both blessing and curse. Blessing because death had stolen Grandmother's other
children. Curse because she feared this child
would be taken, too. She lay awake nights
listening to the child's breathing and wore

her eyes out watching the girl toddle past sharp points and hard surfaces, her breath catching with each stumble.

Wise and quiet as an owl was the baby, and for a time Grandmother thought she should call her daughter Owl. But there was no predator in those eyes, no lust for the kill, only wisdom and forebearing and forgiveness, and Grandmother had called her Red Doe for the time in the spring when the deer are beautiful with the plenty of the land. The name seemed prescient as the girl grew toward womanhood, her step light and gentle on the earth.

In her sixteenth year she brightened the village as the crocus brightens the prairie drab in early spring. Fine-featured and beautiful in the old way, she was, the Cree sense of beauty having been preempted by pale skin and light eyes. But beautiful enough, still, in the white man's way to have caught the attention of some drifters.

She hadn't come home one night, and Grandmother found her by the river, clothing torn from her bruised and bloody body. Aieee, Grandmother thought as she carried the young woman home, those men possessed dark magic, indeed, to turn an act of love into something so brutal and ugly.

Grandmother nursed her daughter for three

days, and when she returned on the fourth day from her snares along the river, Red Doe was gone.

Spring and summer and fall passed, and the white death of winter came visiting. The cold winds flirted with Grandmother, and she with them. And one night after she had been alone longer than anyone was meant to be alone, the Arctic wind sang love songs to her, calling her outside to its icy embrace. She might have gone but for the rapping at the door.

Red Doe, her face so gaunt and ravaged by cold and hunger that a smile would have shattered it, stood on the step. Without speaking, she gently handed a bundle of rags to her mother.

"Call him Judd. Judd was the strongest of the three and took the longest to die. Tell him his father is dead — and his mother."

The door closed then, the scuff of wood against wood submerged in the howl of the Arctic winds and Grandmother's keening.

Judd stood, his chair scraping on the wooden floor.

"I have to go now," he said.

"Where are you going?"

Judd shrugged.

185

"Are you coming back?"

Judd leaned against the table, looking into his grandmother's eyes. "Yes," he said. "I'm coming back."

He stepped toward the door, only to be pulled back by the sound of his grandmother's voice.

"Once when I was a girl in the month when the chokecherries are ripe, I saw a lake where there had never been a lake before. I thought it was a magic lake and thought that I should walk to it and drink of the magic water.

"The sun was so hot the birds hid in the shade of the buffalo berry bushes. I walked and I walked and I walked. But the lake ran ahead of me across the prairie, not even leaving a track, not even a cool breeze from across its waters.

"And then my father galloped up and lifted me to the back of his horse, and I told him about the lake that ran away from me. He said the lake wasn't real. It was just a trick that the sun plays on the people.

"It's hard to tell the difference between magic and tricks."

The old woman nodded then, and made herself invisible in her chair, a clump of rags awaiting Judd's return.

A cloudless sky promised a day ripe with

light and warmth, and Judd walked to the garden. Lines of green rose again between the rail fence the preacher had "paid" them to build.

Judd spat. Paid them with stolen cattle and danger.

But a moment later, the bitterness ebbed, replaced by doubt. If the preacher had been hired by Dirk Newcombe, as Ten Horses said, why was he in jail? Why had no one come to see the people, to tell them they must leave the shacks by the dump?

And if the preacher meant only to help . . . ? Judd shook his head. He didn't want to follow that line of thought. That could only lead him further down the path of despair.

Judd knelt beside the garden, pulling some weeds that had crept into the fertile soil. He was still busy at that when Clinton Old Hawk appeared at the other edge of the garden. Old Hawk stretched and relieved himself before he noticed Judd, then raised his arm in greeting. Judd waved back, and Old Hawk dropped his hoe over the fence and climbed through, working down a row of knee-high corn, cutting weeds and tilling the soil.

Judd grabbed a fence rail and pulled himself to his feet. He stretched then, too, muscles straining as he reached toward the heavens. He waved farewell to Old Hawk and turned toward the river.

It was the month when cottonwoods loose seeds like prayers on sun-warmed air. Judd watched them dance in the heat until a crick in his neck and the brightness of the morning sky forced his eyes to the earth.

The river, raucous and bawdy, staggered between the banks, pushing and shoving at everything in its path.

Judd picked up a flat rock and skipped it across the surface of the stream until a wave lying in wait downstream from a boulder reached up and swallowed it.

He chucked more stones in the river, rewarded only by the *ker-plunk* they made before sinking out of sight.

The boy sighed then and turned toward town. He would likely spend the day as he had spent yesterday and the day before that, hiding in shadows near the jail, afraid to go inside to speak to the preacher, afraid to leave.

Judd wove a circuitous route toward Sanctuary, pausing for a moment within view of the railroad station, seeing in his mind's eye that day a lifetime ago when the preacher stepped off the train. The preacher had changed Judd's life, but the boy didn't know if the change was for better or worse.

He slipped furtively into town, his step tentative, his legs ready for flight, and his eyes darting through backyards and kitchen windows for pale faces and stabbing eyes. Judd thought he was invisible now, but sometimes to move was to be seen and the boy was in too much turmoil to stand still.

Judd slipped into the alley behind the haberdashery and the newspaper. He heard the crunch of shoes against gravel, moving down the narrow space between the two buildings, and his heart jumped. He took a deep breath and stepped into a shadow growing smaller by the moment in the morning sun, hoping it would hide him until the sound and the person who made it went away.

Just as Judd pressed himself into the back wall of the newspaper, a stranger, wrapped in a two-day-old beard and the smell of stale cigar smoke and beer, stepped into the alley. He looked both ways, his eyes flicking across Judd without stopping. Judd's invisibility was holding. The man unbuttoned his pants and relieved himself in the alley, all the while alert.

He buttoned his pants, glanced around again, and then scrunched back through the narrow path between the buildings to the street.

Judd's nose wrinkled at the odor the man

left behind, but he remained hidden in the shadows for several minutes before moving. He crept up the alley, following the path he and the preacher had taken on their way to see Mary Dickens for the first time.

This course took him to Sanctuary's busiest side street, the one leading to the bridge across the Milk. But only a few people walked there in the early-morning light. Judd waited, watching a fly laze about in the early-morning air.

Now! The street was empty.

Judd stepped on the hard-packed clay as he and the preacher had months before, invisible in the full morning light.

A little knot of people had gathered at the Finney house, and Judd smiled at the memory of Mordecai tickling Mrs. Finney on the neck with a feather as she snoozed in her backyard.

He covered his mouth to muffle a chuckle at the thought and stepped nearer to the house, keeping to shadows so he wouldn't be seen.

Doctor Wilson was there, along with the sheriff and a gathering of neighbors. One of the women, hair uncombed and clothing rumpled, stood at the edge of the group, holding her face in her hands as though great pain emanated from it.

"I had just gotten dressed," she said, her

hands gesturing to show the disheveled state of her clothing, "and I was . . . taking my morning walk . . . to the privy.

"Mrs. Finney — isn't it odd, I lived next to her for close to ten years and never did know her first name — was sitting in this old chair next to the fence."

"Emily," the sheriff whispered. "Her name was Emily."

The woman cocked her head, a soft smile crossing her face. "Isn't that pretty." And then the smile disappeared, and the neighbor's lips drew into a thin line.

She sighed before continuing. "She was up at this hour nearly every morning to hang out her wash. Even in the summer she rose before first light.

"She had her first load of wash on the line, and she was just sitting in that chair enjoying the touch of the sun on her face —

"I — " The woman's voice broke then, and sobs shook her body. She wiped her eyes with the back of her hands and took a deep breath.

"I heard her voice, and I thought she was saying something to me, so I stopped, but she wasn't talking to me. She was sitting in her chair and her hand moved to the back of her neck as though she felt something crawling on it.

"And then she said something I couldn't understand — it sounded like 'call of a lovesick moose,' and she laughed."

The woman broke into sobs again, and the sheriff and Doctor Wilson looked away.

"You know, she didn't have much to laugh about, not since her husband died and her children moved away. She's been taking in wash now for years, doing more work than anyone should have to do. But she didn't complain.

"When she laughed, I almost laughed with her. There was so much joy in it. I don't know when I've ever seen her so happy, and then she stopped laughing and fell off the chair . . . and . . . and . . ."

But the woman's voice failed her, lost in the sobs that racked her body.

Sheriff Timothy stepped toward the woman, and Judd instinctively shrank back into the shadows. The boy had been taught to fear this man and the white man law he represented.

But today, the sheriff wrapped his arms — thick as some men's legs — around the woman's shoulders, and she sagged against him, hiding her face and her sobs in her hands.

He helped her through the gate of the Finney property and down along the alley toward her own backyard. That course took him almost within touching distance of Judd, and Judd shrank into the shadows, not breathing.

But the sheriff didn't seem to notice, his attention focused on the woman. At first Judd thought the sheriff was speaking to the woman so softly that only she could understand, but he wasn't speaking. Instead, he was murmuring, making the reassuring noises one might make to a frightened horse.

When the two reached the gate to the woman's backyard, the sheriff stopped and nodded to Doc Wilson and the others, silent and waiting. They slipped away, quiet as clouds.

The air eased out of Judd's lungs, but he didn't move until the alley and the backyard were empty.

Judd drifted up the alley, his mind sifting through what he had just seen. But again and again the image of Mordecai tickling Mrs. Finney's neck with a feather bumped in the boy's mind. The preacher's words that day nagged at Judd: "She deserves one more good laugh before she goes."

Judd squatted in the alley, watching a long trail of ants move mindlessly toward their nest at the edge of the alley. Judd picked up one of the tiny creatures. The ant twisted and squirmed in his fingers, jaws raging helplessly at the huge creature who held it.

Judd dropped the ant and sighed. It was time to go see the preacher.

Judd squatted in the shadow of a cottonwood, hidden behind a bush. Sheriff Timothy was inside. Judd had seen him move past the window, heard the clang of steel against steel as doors opened and closed inside. And now a waitress from the Silver Dollar Saloon stood in front of the jail door. She listed just a bit from the weight of the basket she was carrying, and she shifted it to her other hand before knocking at the door.

A panel in the jail's steel door opened with a click, and a moment later the sheriff invited the waitress inside. The smell of sausage and eggs and biscuits wafted to Judd, and his belly rumbled.

The door swung open again, and the waitress stepped out, leaving the basket and dishes to be picked up later, but still she walked as though she were carrying a heavy burden.

Judd waited until the woman disappeared. He shuddered, then stood, hesitating before leaving the safety of the shadow. He drew a deep breath and crossed the road to the jail, rapping tentatively on the door.

The door opened, and Sheriff Timothy blocked the entrance. "He said you'd be here this morning."

Timothy waved Judd in and stepped over to his desk, rummaging through the papers on it. He picked one up and handed it to Judd.

"Trial starts Monday. This is a subpoena. You've been called as a witness for the prosecution. Report here about a quarter to eight, and I'll take you over."

Judd's eyes were wide with fright, and he was shaking his head.

"No choice, boy. You do what the judge says or he'll hold you in contempt and put you in jail. Neither of us would like that.

"The preacher's eating breakfast now, but I'll take you back." Timothy cocked his head and asked, "You got a gun or a knife?"

Judd shook his head, and Timothy nodded. The sheriff took a ring of keys from a peg on the wall and slipped one into the heavy wooden door leading to the cells. The door slid open on well-oiled hinges, and Judd and the sheriff stepped through.

Mordecai was standing near the door to his cell, his smile lighting the room.

"Judd, I'm so glad you decided to come. I have a lot to talk to you about." Turning his attention to the sheriff, Mordecai asked, "Suppose you could leave the cell door open if I promise not to escape?"

Timothy nodded. "I'll leave the other door

open, too. When you're ready to go, Judd, just come on out."

Judd, his eyes focused on the floor, nodded.

The sheriff stepped out of the cell block, and Mordecai waved Judd into the cell.

"Never known you not to be hungry," Mordecai said. "I wasn't hungry this morning, so I've got eggs and hash browns and sausage and toast.

"Sit down and help yourself."

Judd shook his head, and Mordecai's voice dropped.

"Go ahead, boy. It's a shame to waste food when so many people are hungry."

Judd was famished. He sat on the bed, the metal jail tray on his lap, and ate the eggs and toast, eyeing the link sausage. He tried hard to eat slowly, to postpone what he had to say, but the taste of the eggs and potatoes and buttered toast pulled him through the meal.

When he stopped eating there was still a knot in his stomach, brought on, he thought, by the aroma of the sausage still lying on his plate. He wrapped the links in his handkerchief and put them in his shirt pocket.

"For your grandmother?" Mordecai asked, and when Judd nodded, the preacher smiled. "You'll do all right."

Judd sat silently on the bed, staring at

196

the floor, and then he spoke. "Mrs. Finney died. A neighbor said she had her 'last laugh' about the moose call just like you said."

"She was a good woman," Mordecai replied.

"How did you know about her last laugh?"

"Judd, she was old and tired. She could have gone any time."

Judd looked at the preacher, staring into his eyes. His voice dropped to a whisper. "I have to tell you something." He took a deep breath and let it go, hissing between his teeth.

He continued, "I was the one who told the sheriff you rustled the cattle. I thought the people would be blamed if I didn't. I thought we would all go to jail."

Judd sighed, and his voice broke. "I wanted the money, too. And I thought that maybe Jack was right, that you were working with Mr. Newcombe. I thought you had sold us for money, so it wouldn't matter if I sold you."

Judd looked up at the preacher, a sheen of tears on his face.

"But that isn't true, is it? You aren't working with Mr. Newcombe."

The preacher sat on the bed and put an arm around Judd.

"No, that isn't true."

"Then, I have done a terrible thing." Judd's

voice was coming between sobs. "And the sheriff gave me a piece of paper that says I have to be in court Monday, or the judge will hold me in contempt and put me in jail."

"I didn't know they put you in jail for contempt."

Mordecai hugged Judd, tears running down his face and dripping into the boy's hair.

Thirteen

The Reverend Eli crawled from the galvanized tub, stepping to a towel spread on the kitchen floor. He stood there naked, water dripping from his body, arms raised in prayer.

"Father, cleanse me for this battle which is about to ensue. Wash away the filth of earth and mankind, and let me shine with the light of my special purity." He was breathing deeply and his thoughts turned to Naomi Parkman, but he shook his head. He must focus his whole being on the task before him today.

He dressed slowly and carefully, donning his best black suit and starched shirt, running a cloth again over his shoes, buffing them until they shone like a black mirror. Then he set his freshly brushed, flat-brimmed black hat on his head, straightening it in the mirror.

He smoothed his coat over his chest and hips and smiled at the image. He was ready.

Puffs of dust marked the Reverend's steps as he crossed the street, ignoring traffic and passersby. The Elder Jackson stopped his wagon to let the Reverend pass, cursing under

his breath after his Christian act went un-
noticed.

The Reverend sought shade as he walked
toward the jail, preferring it to the hot June
sun. When he reached the sheriff's office,
he knocked impatiently. The panel in the
door clicked open, and Deputy Abner peeked
out, rushing to open the door when he saw
who was waiting.

The deputy's mind was scurrying even
faster than his feet. Abner knew that one
word from the Reverend's pulpit would do
his campaign for sheriff a lot of good.

"Sheriff Timothy's out having coffee at
the Silver Dollar. Seems like whenever
anything's happening, he's down there,"
Abner said, pausing to watch his visitor's
reaction as the Reverend stepped in.

When the Reverend did not respond, Abner
worried that the Reverend would take the
comment wrong. He had a tendency to look
on the dark side of things. Probably some
verse or another in the Bible about not telling
tales about your boss when you're running
for his job, and that damn Reverend knew
the good book by rote.

Abner was angry at himself for mouthing
off like that about the sheriff. On the other
hand, what made the Reverend so high and
mighty? What the hell made the Reverend

think he could pick Sanctuary's sheriff?

Abner's growing rancor poked out of his voice. "Well, what can I do for you, *Reverend?*"

"I came to see this man they call preacher."

"He's got a visitor right now."

"I'll take care of that," the Reverend said, leaving Abner fuming in his wake.

Mordecai and Judd were sitting on the cot, Mordecai with his arm around Judd's shoulders.

The Reverend's lip curled. "I'm not surprised to find a heathen with you."

Mordecai cocked his head and stared at the Reverend Eli for a moment. "You'd best be going," he whispered to Judd. "Come back and see me tomorrow."

Judd darted from the cell and ran to the back door of the jail rather than pass within arm's reach of that man clad in black. He slipped the bolt in the door and fled into the alley.

"What can I do for you?" Mordecai asked.

The Reverend sneered. "That's the question, isn't it?"

"Maybe you can make yourself a little plainer."

"You know what I mean."

The preacher swept his arm around the empty cell. "As you can see, I'm a busy man. I don't have much time for guessing games."

"I have fasted for three days," the Reverend said.

"Good for you."

The Reverend's face wrinkled in conjecture.

Mordecai continued, "If I'm expected to play a role in this little drama, you ought to fill me in on my part."

"Your role is no secret to you. If you choose not to tempt me, I must assume that you realize I cannot be tempted, that I am my Father's son."

"Yes," Mordecai whispered. "You are your father's son. Your father was a drunkard and a wastrel who bedded both you and your sisters when you were but children."

"No!" The Reverend's denial reverberated through the jail as though it had been beaten on a drum. His eyes were wide and rolling, and his head shaking in disavowal. "No! That man was not my father."

"And you are visiting the sins of your father on the children of your congregations."

The Reverend's face blanched white.

"You came here to be tempted, Reverend, so I'll tempt you. Drop to your knees now and pray to God for the forgiveness of your sins. Ask Him to forgive you your hubris and intemperance and intolerance. Ask Him to make well all those you have corrupted with your hate and lust. Ask Him how you may serve His purpose on earth and not your own. And then beg forgiveness of Judd and his people, the people of your congregation, the people of Sanctuary, and all the people you have touched with your special brand of evil. Throw yourself on the mercy of man and God.

"Do that, Brother Eli, and I will pray with you for God's forgiveness, and perhaps He will make you whole again."

The Reverend Eli recoiled from Mordecai's words. He staggered back as though he had been struck a killing blow. He came to rest against the jail wall, where he squirmed, as if trying to force himself through it, to escape Mordecai's eyes.

Then, as Mordecai watched, the Reverend Eli began to change. His face was pressed in profile against the wall, but he stared at Mordecai from the corner of his eye. Color rushed back into his face until it glowed a dull red, hot with the fires that burned within. Sweat trickled down his face and dropped off his chin, the sparse fat of his body rendering with the heat.

When he spoke, his voice was low and contained and deadly.

"You are subtle, deceiver, much more subtle than the last time we met. But you cannot promise me salvation. Salvation is not yours to give."

"I did not promise — "

"Oh, you're subtle, Satan — subtle in the ways that you would confuse me, but I have denied your temptations once again. I have proven myself stronger than you."

The Reverend's eyes were wide, staring. "And now you will face me in the Holocaust, and I will defeat you and sit in judgment upon your kind. Expect no mercy from me, Satan. Expect only hellfire and the pain of burning forever without the respite of death. I will put you on a spit and watch you roast."

Spittle was now dripping from the corners of the Reverend's mouth.

"Once you have been convicted of rustling, no one will ever believe you. They will join me and march against your army of evil, and I will TRIUMPH!"

That word boomed through the jail until it seemed that the windows rattled with it.

Deputy Abner, obviously shaken, suddenly appeared at the door.

"Uh, Reverend, it might be a good idea if you were to go now. The sheriff's coming, and . . . well . . . you know how he is."

The Reverend Eli turned his wild, terrible eyes on the deputy, and Abner flinched.

"The reckoning will come soon enough,"

the Reverend said, "for those who oppose me." He marched through the door.

He would speak to his congregation Sunday, warn them of the evil among them. He would set fire to their faith, build a conflagration big enough to burn this blasphemer's soul.

By Monday when the trial was due to begin, the so-called preacher would know what it was to face the wrath of the righteous.

Fourteen

The crowd converged on the courthouse before eight o'clock, little knots of people braiding together as neatly and orderly as macramé.

Some came because the Reverend Eli told them to come, to sit in judgment on this evil man posing as a believer. Others were curious, spilling out of watering holes and kitchens because entertainment was dear in Sanctuary.

The prospective jurors were easy to pick out of the crowd. They stood stiffly in starched shirts and Sunday-go-to-meeting suits, nodding ceremoniously at others, speaking in hushed tones. They stood on the courthouse steps, waiting for Melvin Jacobs, the clerk of court, to open the door.

Jacobs, punctual and punctilious, opened county business promptly at eight, and closed promptly at five — crowds and county business not so important as the minute hand on his gold hunter's watch.

Inside, Jacobs appeared at one minute to eight and stood clearly visible through the windows in the courthouse doors. The clerk ignored the waiting throng, focusing his attention on his watch, instead. At exactly eight, the latch on the door clicked opened and the crowd filed past the clerk's slightly disapproving gaze.

Heels clicked across marble flooring a Great Falls architect had sold the commissioners after a long night of buying drinks at the Silver Dollar, spinning alcoholic fantasies of Sanctuary's future. The clicks echoed through the cool, cavernous hall, changing to thumps as the crowd filed up dark-stained oak stairs to the second floor.

The door to the courtroom was locked, and the crowd stood milling in the hall. The door clicked open and Jacobs, having entered the courtroom through the judge's chambers, stood in the entrance.

"Prospective jurors first," he said. As the crowd shuffled into order, Jacobs continued. "All jurors will be paid, chosen or not, for appearing this morning. Simply present yourself to my office, and my assistant will provide the three dollars daily stipend due you. Those of you who have come from out of town to answer the summons will receive an additional ten cents per mile for travel to and from Sanctuary.

"After the trial ends, the jury will be sequestered. Does anyone here not understand 'sequestered'?"

The jurors fidgeted, but no one spoke.

Jacobs' lip curled. "Let me put that another way. Does anyone here know what sequestered means?"

Silence.

Jacobs' eyes rolled heavenward. "I thought not. Sequestered means that you will retire for deliberation until you have reached a decision.

"That means you won't be able to go home for dinner unless you decide the case in a hurry. Do you understand that?"

The jurors nodded.

"Good. Take the first two pews at the front on the right. You must be sitting in alphabetical order. I'll help you with that. The front pew on the left is reserved for witnesses and Mr. Topple of the *Sanctuary Bugle*. Do you understand?"

The jurors nodded again. The trial of the preacher Mordecai was about to begin.

Judd rose before the sun cracked the eastern horizon. He stepped outside the shack, careful as he opened the door to not awaken his grandmother. He stretched in the cool morning air kissed by snowfields still covering the Rockies to the west.

He stretched again, picked up a bent, galvanized bucket and walked up the hill toward the slaughterhouse, the rusty bail creaking in cadence with his steps.

The slaughterhouse pump screeched in protest as Judd pulled on the handle with both arms, and the boy hoped the sound would not awaken anyone in the village.

When the bucket was full, Judd leaned into it, bracing it against his leg as he hobbled down the hill, the bucket's bail cutting into his fingers, water splashing on his leg whenever he stumbled.

He set the bucket on the step while he opened the door, rubbing his hands to take some of the ache from the red line that cut across his fingers. Then he lifted the bucket to the rickety table beside the stove, muttering as the table sagged under the weight and water sloshed over the edge. The washbasin, rusted where the enamel had chipped off, clattered as he set it on the stove, and Judd grimaced, hoping the sound would not poke into Grandmother's sleep.

He stripped off his clothes and washed himself from head to foot, scrubbing with a clean rag and shivering a little as the water touched him. Then he pulled on the shirt and trousers Doc had bought him for the trial.

The shirt and trousers — the first new clothing Judd had worn in his twelve years — felt stiff and scratchy. The shoes, shiny, black, and laced to his ankles, rubbed against his feet, the leather hard and unyielding.

He had taken the packages from Doc with wonder in his eyes, and the old man turned to hide his face when Judd tried to thank him.

Still, Judd didn't want to be seen in the village dressed in such finery when others had so little, so he pointed his feet toward Sanctuary.

Puffs of dust rose with each step to settle on his new shoes, dulling the shiny black finish. It was time to answer the call of that piece of paper the sheriff had given him last week.

Judd lined up at the door of the courtroom, the other witnesses towering over him and the words of the bailiff a blur in his ears.

". . . Called to the chair beside the judge's bench . . . Oath administered . . . Collect fee at the clerk of court's office . . . Don't talk to each other about the case . . ."

The heavy oak door swung open. All the faces in the court swiveled toward the witnesses, and Judd gasped. He felt immersed in the scrutiny, unable to breathe.

And then the line was moving and Judd moved with it, borne helpless into the courtroom as though a vortex were sucking him down into its depths. He drew a deep breath and plunged.

Judd was first in line, and Jacobs was waiting to direct the witnesses into the correct seats. He pointed Judd toward the far end of the bench.

Judd huddled into the corner, trying vainly to meld himself into the wood. The room was thick with the odor of sweaty wool, mothballs, old varnish, and morbid curiosity. He was sitting directly below one of the windows lining the south wall of the courtroom, and Judd would gladly have risked the two-story jump to the ground below if only he could escape.

He slouched in his seat, trying to hide from the eyes burning into the back of his neck. No longer invisible, he was trapped here in full view of the people of Sanctuary.

He saw the preacher enter, glance around the courtroom, and smile as his eyes met Judd's. But he was no help now, seated with his broad back turned on Judd and on the people of Sanctuary.

Judge William Tecumseh Harding fidgeted in the chair that better fit the bottom of its normal occupant, Judge Harvey Jenkins, than his own. Jenkins had written, asking Harding to hear this case. Trying a preacher for rustling beef from the biggest rancher in the county was fraught with political danger, and

Jenkins intended to retire with his job intact.

It wasn't the first time the two judges had traded places, and Harding liked to keep his credit good in case a similar situation arose in his own district. He turned his attention to the trial.

The selection of the jury had gone well. Short questions and no objections. The preacher had elected to represent himself. Harding had tried to talk him out of that foolishness, but Mordecai wouldn't listen.

There was justice in that, Harding thought: he hadn't spent much time listening to preachers, either.

Without a defense attorney, the trial would likely go pretty fast, and that suited the judge just fine.

Biggest crowd he'd seen at a trial in some time. The Reverend Eli had been out stirring up his parishioners. They had the look of vengeance in their eyes, and a tiny shudder ran down Harding's back. Good defense attorney could have gotten a change of venue, but . . . Harding sighed and raised his gavel. Time to get this circus under way.

"Your Honor, the prosecution calls Jack Ranking."

The crowd had come to watch justice done, and ordinarily County Attorney Thomas

Driscoll would have relished the opportunity to strut his piece before a crowd of electors. But this case rippled the hair on the back of his neck. It seemed too easy. No defense attorney, no question which way the jury was leaning — especially those who were members of the Reverend Eli's congregation — and the case was woven together like a fine wool coat.

But it had been Driscoll's experience that when everything fit together too easily, that was when it was most likely to unravel.

The first witness, Jack Ranking, was called. Judd, head bent and unmoving, followed Ranking to the stand with his eyes.

The Bar Nothing cowboy was dressed in his Saturday night best, boots thumping awkwardly on the floor with the stiff-legged gait of a man more accustomed to riding than walking.

Ranking squirmed in the chair. He clearly didn't like courtrooms — his previous experience limited to drunk-and-disorderly charges. He didn't like being in a room full of people unless the room had liquor and a piano player. Moreover, he didn't like people who wore ties.

Driscoll pried the story from the taciturn cowboy. Ranking had been riding fence when he noticed that the barbed wire had been dropped over a twenty-foot section and then tacked back up. Cattle had been driven through the opening by one man on horseback, Ranking said.

"Did you try to follow those tracks?" Driscoll asked.

"No, sir," Ranking replied.

"What did you do?"

"I checked to see that the fence was tight so no cattle would wander away and high-tailed it back to the Bar Nothing to tell Mr. Newcombe what I had seen."

"And what had you seen?"

Ranking looked at Driscoll as though the question were too foolish to answer.

"Rustling," he said, provocation poking out of his voice. "I saw where somebody had rustled Bar Nothing beef."

Murmurs rippled through the crowd.

Mordecai rose for the cross-examination, and Judd wondered at the preacher's composure in this sea of rancor.

"Mr. Ranking, how did you know the cattle had been rustled?"

Ranking bristled. "The fence was down and the cattle were gone."

"Have you ever seen cattle cross a downed fence before without being rustled?"

"Not with a horse behind them."

"Was somebody on that horse?"

"How the hell should I know?"

"That's the point, Mr. Ranking. That's the point. Your honor, I ask the court to strike Mr. Ranking's statement that the cattle had been rustled. At this point he can establish nothing more than that cattle *appeared* to be missing."

Driscoll was on his feet. "Your Honor — "

"Motion granted. The court reporter will strike Mr. Ranking's conjecture that the cattle had been rustled. That has not yet been established."

Judge Harding leaned back in his chair. So the preacher had been in court before, Harding surmised. This case might be interesting after all.

Red was creeping up under Driscoll's collar, but his voice was contained. "The state calls Dirk Newcombe, Your Honor."

Newcombe stumped to the witness chair, the wildness and injuries of his youth putting a hitch into each step, each swing of his arms. He raised his hand to take the oath and said "I do" at the correct time, but his eyes were poking holes into the preacher.

Driscoll began his questioning.

"Mr. Newcombe, when did you first learn of the rustl — "

Mordecai rose. "Your Honor — "

"Objection sustained. Mr. Driscoll, you will

refrain from making any reference to rustling until it has, in fact, been established that there was rustling."

"Yes, Your Honor."

Driscoll took a deep breath and began again. "Mr. Newcombe, when were you first aware that your cattle were missing?"

"Objection, Your Honor." Mordecai took two steps toward the judge's bench. "We have not yet established that any of Mr. Newcombe's cattle are missing."

"The hell we haven't!" Newcombe stood so fast the witness chair skittered backward and tipped over. "Those cows were rustled, and you did it."

The judge's gavel hit the stand before Mordecai could voice his objection.

"Mr. Newcombe, you will take your seat and reply only to questions asked you by counsel."

"Bullshit!" Newcombe's face was livid. "No two-bit judge is going to tell me what I can do and what I can't. You want to keep your plush job," Newcombe roared, "you'll stop this dillydallying and get the job done. I've got more important things to do."

Color was rising now under Judge Harding's collar.

"Mr. Newcombe," Harding growled. "You

may be bull goose in Sanctuary, but you are subject to the same law as everyone else. You will sit down and confine your speeches to answering questions, or I will hold you in contempt. I don't think you'd like sitting in a jail cell until I decide you're fit to get out."

"I've been in jails before."

"I'm sure you have. Now sit down!"

Newcombe sat down on the edge of the witness chair, back straight as a post, eyes burning in the shadows beneath his heavy brows.

Driscoll avoided looking into Newcombe's eyes.

"Mr. Newcombe, what did you do when Mr. Ranking showed you the downed fence and the tracks of the cattle?"

"Fence wasn't down then, it was back up."

"But you could see that it had been taken down?"

The muscles knotted in Newcombe's jaw.

"Never saw cows walk through a fence before and leave it standing."

An uneasy titter ran through the crowd, and Newcombe glared at the bobbing heads.

"Mr. Newcombe, did you have any cattle in that pasture that were not your own?"

Newcombe's fist knotted, and he leaned forward to rise. "You calling me a rustler?"

Driscoll blanched.

"No," he stuttered. "Certainly not, but

217

sometimes cattlemen lease grazing rights or let their hands run a few head."

"I don't!" Newcombe growled, one lid crawling down his eye.

"No offense, Mr. Newcombe. I just wanted to establish that those were, in fact, your cattle."

"They were my cattle."

"And what did you do then?"

"Tried to track them."

"Did you have any success?"

"Rustler drove them up or down the Milk. The tracks were all washed out."

"Did you find anything else?"

"Found an Indian camp just across the Milk."

"How do you know it was an Indian camp?"

Newcombe cocked his head and glowered at Driscoll. When he spoke it was through clenched teeth. "I saw my first Indian camp before you were born. I know an Indian camp when I see it."

Driscoll stepped back from the force of Newcombe's eyes.

"And what did you do then?" Driscoll asked, his voice barely more than a whisper.

"Sent one of the boys in to tell Sheriff Timothy, not that I expected that lard-gut to do anything about it."

Timothy was sitting just in front of Judd, his chair leaning back on two legs against the wall. As Newcombe spoke, the chair eased forward to rest on all four legs. Color spread across the sheriff's face, and Judd could see the sheen of sweat on Timothy's forehead and the knots in the muscles of his jaw.

The sheriff rose then and opened the window beside Judd, and the boy drank deeply of the cool air that swept through.

"That's all the questions I have, Your Honor," Driscoll said, slumping into his chair.

Mordecai rose.

"How many cattle do you have in that pasture, Mr. Newcombe?"

Newcombe glared at Mordecai, the silence filling the room to the detonation point. But when he spoke his voice was flat as two-day-old beer.

"Three hundred fifty, maybe four hundred head."

"How many cattle do you think moved across that fence, judging by the tracks?"

"Figure ten, maybe fifteen head."

"How many horses do you have?"

Newcombe's eyes disappeared into slits. In Montana, strangers do not ask a man how many acres he owns or how much stock he runs on it.

But Newcombe answered. "About a hundred twenty head."

"Are there any horses in that pasture?"

Newcombe hesitated. "Might be."

"Why was Mr. Ranking riding fence?"

"Because I told him to."

"Why did you tell him to?"

Exasperation cracked through Newcombe's voice. "To check the fence."

"Because fence staples rust and posts rot and sometimes cattle rub against the posts and break them?"

Newcombe nodded.

"And why do you have fences, Mr. Newcombe?"

Newcombe cranked a glaring eye on Mordecai and reached for the railing around the witness box to pull himself to his feet. "Why the hell should I answer these stupid damn questions?"

Harding leaned down from the bench and fixed Newcombe with an equally glaring eye. "Because if you don't, I'll toss you in jail."

"I have fences to keep my cattle on my land," Newcombe spat.

"And to keep other ranchers' cattle off your land?"

"Hell, yes!"

"And sometimes the fences go down, and your cattle wander off and other cattle wander onto Bar Nothing grass."

Newcombe's voice rumbled like a coffeepot on a hot stove. "Those sonsabitches would all run their cattle on the Bar Nothing if I didn't keep the fences up."

"So if I can summarize your testimony, Mr. Newcombe, cattle that may or may not have been your own were either driven or wandered off your ranch, and you have been unable to find them. Is that right, Mr. Newcombe?"

"No, that is not right! You rustled my beef, and I'll see you pay for it if it's the last thing I do!"

Mordecai's voice came like a bucket of water on a wildfire.

"And how do you know that was an Indian camp across the river?"

Newcombe was on his feet. "By the smell," he roared. "By the stink of 'em. Just like the stink of that one!"

Newcombe's finger settled on Judd's forehead.

Judd, eyes wide with terror, tried to sink down in his seat, to make himself invisible. He felt as though he were shriveling, becoming a husk. He wanted to say that he had washed this morning as he always did. He wanted to say that he was wearing new clothing that smelled more of the store than him. But he was speechless, terror-stricken. His eyes moved pleading to Mordecai.

When Mordecai spoke, the jury had to strain to hear him. "That's all the questions I have, Your Honor."

Harding turned to Driscoll. "Does the prosecution have any more questions?"

Driscoll shook his head.

"You are excused, Mr. Newcombe."

Newcombe scowled at the judge, but he held his tongue. Two weeks in jail and those thieving cowmen who ringed his place like vultures would steal him blind. Had to watch them all the time. He picked the scuffed, dirty hat from his lap, jammed it over his ears, and stood.

Then in a voice coarse as gravel on a Milk River bar, he growled, "Come on, boys. The drinks are on me. I want to wash the stink of this place off me."

Newcombe glared once more at the judge, retribution promised in every inch of his body, then strode out of the courtroom, too proud to yield to the pain that each step drove into his brain.

The door creaked shut on the last Bar Nothing cowhand, and the courtroom was awash in silence. When Driscoll released the air trapped in his lungs, the sound could be heard three rows back.

"I would like to call Sheriff Timothy," he croaked.

Timothy took the oath and squeezed into a witness chair too confining for his bulk.

Yes, he had been in his office when the Bar Nothing cowboy reported the rustling. Yes, he had investigated. No, he had not been able to develop a case until a witness had stepped forward.

"Is that witness in the courtroom?"

Timothy nodded and pointed to Judd.

"Since you arrested the preacher Mordecai, have you done any further investigation?"

"Yes."

"And what did you hope to discover?"

"To check the validity of the witness's story, and to further determine the preacher Mordecai's identity."

"And what did that investigation reveal?"

"The witness's story could be corroborated, but I could not verify the preacher's identity. He wouldn't give me his last name, and I could find records of only two people named Mordecai graduating from seminaries representing the major denominations. One died of natural causes some years ago in — Timothy checked his notes — Paris, Missouri. The other died in Enid, Oklahoma.

"He was hanged," Timothy said. "He was hanged by the neck until dead."

Fifteen

"The prosecution calls Judd Medicine Elk."

Judd sat terrified, knuckles white on the railing before him.

County Attorney Thomas Driscoll turned to look at the boy. "Your Honor, the prosecution calls Judd Medicine Elk."

Judd pulled himself to his feet and sidled along the bench, steadying himself with the rail, steadying himself with the forgiveness in the preacher's eyes.

The courtroom was walled in a palpable silence broken only by the rustle of new clothing and the beat of Judd's heart. *Thump! Thump! Thump!* It echoed in the boy's ears loud as the drums that day of the village feast.

Judd would gladly have stopped that pounding, exhaled his last breath, if he could. Everyone in the courtroom was looking at him, and he wilted under their glare, as a cut flower wilts in the sun.

Drops of sweat trickled down his neck. The boy was afraid that the jurors would wrinkle their noses at the stink of him.

Judd had tried to imagine foulness strong enough to twist Dirk Newcombe's face into such revulsion he had seen earlier. Perhaps the stench was as bad as that of the horse. . . .

The horse lay in a cloud of flies on the bank of the Milk, empty eye sockets staring reproachfully as Judd neared. He peered at the animal for a moment, wondering at the spark of life that had once made this rotting flesh dance across the prairie, wondering where that spark had gone when the horse closed its empty eyes. On a whim, he had tried to lift one of the horse's legs, but it had fallen off, revealing a body full of writhing maggots. The stench had been unbearable. . . .

But even that had not twisted his face as Newcombe's had twisted this day on the witness stand when he spoke of the foulness of Judd and the people.

Judd knew from that fierce look that the stink was bone deep; that he would never rid himself of it. He knew, too, that the stink came from the acrid redolence of the dump, that he was steeped in it, as a ham is steeped in the smoke of a curing fire.

The clerk's voice rumbled but Judd couldn't pull meaning from the sound. He knew that he should say "I do," so he did, his voice little more than a squeak. He sat in the witness chair, pulling his body into itself, confining his rankness to as small a space as possible.

"Would you please state your full name for the court?"

"Judd Medicine Elk," Judd whispered.

"You will have to speak louder so the jury can hear you," Thomas Driscoll said softly. He nodded, and Judd repeated his name a little louder.

"And where do you live?"

Tears welled in the boy's eyes, but he turned his face to stone and dammed the flow. "I live at the dump."

"Who do you live with?"

"Grandmother."

"Where are your mother and father?"

"Dead."

"Does anyone else live at the dump?"

"Yes."

"And who are they?"

"The people."

"The people?"

"Yes."

"And who are the people?"

Judd looked at Driscoll, bewilderment plain in his eyes.

"Are they Indians, too?" Driscoll asked.

"Yes."

"Do you know the defendant?"

Again, the baffled look.

Driscoll rephrased his question. "Do you know the preacher Mordecai?"

"Yes."

"And did you tell the sheriff that you thought the preacher had stolen Mr. Newcombe's cattle?"

"Yes," Judd whispered, and the dam broke and a tear trickled down his cheek and dripped off his chin. "I did that."

"What led you to believe that?"

And Judd haltingly told the jury about the night Jasper and the others had driven Bar Nothing cattle across the garden and that the preacher had promised them meat to cure for the winter if they would replant the garden and build a fence around it.

And when the garden was replanted and the fence built, the preacher had led them down the Milk to the killing place, and the people had found ten steers hanging from the cottonwoods. Judd, eyes fixed on Driscoll, told him about seeing tracks across the river and wading over to find where the fence had been let down and the cattle driven across.

A murmur ran through the courtroom, and Driscoll said, "That's all the questions I have of this witness, Your Honor."

Mordecai rose and walked to the witness box.

"Could you tell how old those tracks were, Judd?"

Judd shook his head.

"Did you see any tracks on the other side of the river where the cattle had been driven out of the water?"

Reflection crossed Judd's face. He shook his head again.

"Were there any entrails or hides or heads in the camp?"

Judd said, "No."

"I have no further questions, Your Honor."

Judge Harding nodded to Driscoll. "Any more questions before I excuse this witness?"

Driscoll stood.

"Did you scout the banks to find out where these 'wandering' cattle" — he turned to the jury and rolled his eyes heavenward — "might have crossed the river?"

Judd shook his head, but then as Driscoll turned to take his seat, Judd remembered something that seemed odd at the time, but that he had not thought about until this moment. He was torn between his need to escape the witness box and his need to purge himself, to tell everything he knew.

"I saw wagon tracks," Judd said, "around the camp."

Driscoll jerked, before turning to Judge

Harding. "The prosecution rests its case, Your Honor."

Harding nodded, and said, "The defense may call its first witness."

Mordecai stood. "Your honor, I am the only witness I intend to call. If Mr. Driscoll has no objections, I would like to dispense with the question-and-answer format and simply state my case in a narrative fashion."

"I have no objection, Your Honor."

Mordecai was sworn in and began. "I don't dispute any of the facts presented by earlier witnesses. I did, in fact, take the cattle from the Bar Nothing ranch."

Again a murmur rumbled through the crowd, and Judge Harding raised his gavel.

"I do, however, take issue with the opinions given here as evidence. I did not 'rustle' those cattle. I bought them."

The murmur broke into a roar, and the judge's gavel cracked through the courtroom. "Order! There will be order in this court."

"Mr. Medicine Elk's testimony," Mordecai said with a nod in Judd's direction, "is true. I did offer the people meat in return for replanting the garden and for building a sturdy fence around it.

"And I did, in fact, inquire at the slaughterhouse as to the possibility of acquiring that meat. I was told that while they were expecting a delivery from the Bar Nothing, they had no beef for butchering at that time. Mr. Hennessey, who works at the slaughterhouse, can corroborate that statement if the court and Mr. Driscoll consider it necessary. Mr. Hennessey happens to be working today and would be available at only a few minutes' notice.

"My experience with Mr. Newcombe is that he does most of his 'business' at night. In keeping with his own practice, I went out that night and took delivery of the cattle myself. I herded them up the Milk and across the river bottom, leaving them corralled at the slaughterhouse until the following morning when they were butchered.

"Then I hauled the carcasses by wagon to the killing place and called upon the people of the village to take delivery of the meat.

"I would like to enter into evidence, your honor, my bill of sale for the purchase of ten butchered steers, and my receipt for the wagon I used to haul the beef to the killing place. Please note that the bill of sale is marked 'paid in advance.'"

Mordecai stepped up to the bench and handed two pieces of paper to Judge Harding. Driscoll, face white as Mordecai's receipt, jumped from his chair and rushed to the bench.

Harding asked, "Mr. Driscoll, do you have any objection?"

Driscoll had a plethora of objections. He objected to being dragged through this farce of a trial. He objected to laying his political future on the line for what was obviously some ploy of the preacher's. He objected to the humiliation he had suffered at the hands of Dirk Newcombe.

But the receipts were valid. Driscoll knew that to be a certainty. He shook his head, trying to find a new line.

Judge Harding hid a grin behind his hand. When word got around that Dirk Newcombe tried to pin rustling charges on a man who bought Bar Nothing beef, he'd be the laughingstock of eastern Montana. Serve the son-of-a-bitch right.

"The clerk will enter the receipts into evidence," Harding said. "Please mark them One-A and Two-A."

Mordecai turned to the judge. "Your Honor, I rest my case."

Harding nodded. The trial had gone even better than he had expected. If they worked through the lunch hour, he might be able to catch the afternoon train home and sleep in his own bed tonight, not the lumpy contraption in the hotel.

"If the prosecution has no questions of

this witness, we will continue with the final arguments. Would the clerk please make arrangements for lunch to be served to the jurors after they retire?"

Melvin Jacobs nodded, but he wasn't happy about the decision. He had planned to have lunch for the jurors at twelve noon. Now, he would have to change his plans for the judge's convenience. He rolled his eyes. Just one thing after another.

Driscoll stood to fight for his political life. "Gentlemen of the jury," he began. "I'm surprised that you haven't been forced to tie bandannas over your noses to protect your lungs from the smoke Mr. — uh — Mordecai has pumped into the courtroom.

"He would have you believe that the fact that he may, or may not, have bought the steers he delivered to the — uh — Indians ameliorates his guilt in this case. Nothing could be further from the truth.

"The facts are quite simple. Mr. Mordecai comes into Sanctuary from only God knows where. None of us knows what secrets he might have left behind him, secrets so terrible that he would refuse even to reveal his name for fear that we might discover them."

"*Mr. Driscoll!*" Judge Harding spat the name as though it were a bug that had flown into his mouth. "You are an attorney at the bar of the state of Montana. You know better than to breach the rules of this court, planting wild conjecture in the minds of this jury.

"You will confine your remarks to the evidence at hand. Do you understand me, sir?"

A stain of red crept across the back of Driscoll's neck; he wilted visibly under the heat of Harding's remark. "Yes, Your Honor."

Driscoll cleared his throat. "The facts in this case are simple. But first we must discuss what we don't know.

"We don't know how many cattle were taken. Mr. Newcombe estimated that he had lost between ten and fifteen head.

"We don't know where those cattle were taken, and we don't know if the cattle the preacher brought to the slaughterhouse were the same animals taken from the ranch."

Judge Harding stood, back stiff as the gavel in his hand. "There is one more thing we don't know, Mr. Driscoll. We don't know why you continue to try to plant speculation in the minds of the jury. The defendant can be found guilty only by that which we *do* know. Let's get on with that. The jury is instructed to ignore Mr. Driscoll's earlier statements." The judge sat down, glowering at the prosecutor.

Driscoll pulled a handkerchief from his

pocket and wiped his forehead. When he spoke, his voice seemed broken, the words poking through his trepidation like bits of ice floating down a river.

"We do know the preacher Mordecai admits to having gone on Bar Nothing land to take cattle pastured there without the knowledge or permission of the owner. That's all you need to know to find the preacher guilty.

"Thank you for your attention during the trial." Driscoll smiled wanly at the jury and sat down.

Mordecai rose.

"No," he said, his voice soft as a spring rain. "That isn't all you need to know.

"You need to know why I went such a roundabout way to buy cattle for the people of that little settlement down by the dump. I'd like to tell you about that.

"Dirk Newcombe has a soul-deep hatred for the Indian people. Most of you probably don't know this, but Mr. Newcombe lost his wife to a marauding band of Blackfeet only a couple of years after he drove his longhorns into this country.

"The pall of black smoke that hangs occasionally over Sanctuary comes from fires at the slaughterhouse, where Mr. Newcombe has decided that he would rather burn livers and hearts and kidneys than to *sell* them to the Cree and Métis in the village.

"It is not often that conviction gets in the way of profit, but Mr. Newcombe's hatred is deeper than even his pocketbook. I didn't consider it likely that he would go out of his way to sell me beef which I would then give to the people.

"So I bought the cattle that afternoon at the slaughterhouse and took delivery that night on the Bar Nothing. Since the butchers expected a delivery of beef, they didn't question finding the animals in the corral. Since I took all those animals after they were slaughtered, the butchers didn't question the fact that more steers showed up later."

Mordecai's voice dropped to a whisper. "And since Mr. Newcombe had already set a precedent for herding cattle to slaughter in the darkest hours of the night, they didn't question that either.

"Those are the reasons I took those cattle from the Bar Nothing."

Mordecai walked back to the table for the defense and poured a glass of water from a pitcher there. He drank it and turned again to face the jury.

"It seems to me there are two more questions that need to be cleared up.

"Why did I wait for the trial rather than

show the receipts to the sheriff? First, I thought I had a better chance of pleading my case before a jury than pleading it before Dirk Newcombe. His behavior in the courtroom vindicates my judgment. Second, I wanted a chance to talk with you in a neutral environment, away from the banging drums of the 'Christian soldiers' and the stridency of the Reverend Eli Timpkins."

A murmur ran through the courtroom. The trial could turn out to be a showdown between the preacher and the Reverend. Members of the Church of Righteousness stiffened their backs. The Reverend had warned them of the battle. Other townsfolk hid grins of anticipation. The preacher Mordecai was no pushover. Could be they were about to witness a first-class fight.

Eyes jerked to the Reverend Eli. The muscles of his jaws were knotted and his face was tinged deep red. His mouth was a thin line, tight with the effort of holding it closed.

Mordecai continued. "There is one point on which I must agree with Mr. Newcombe. The moment I stepped off the train in Sanctuary, I realized there is a godawful stench here."

Judd slipped down even farther into his seat. He had been the first person the preacher had seen in Sanctuary. He had been waiting at the station, staining the air with his stink.

Judd could feel the eyes and the contempt of the audience on his back. He wished that he could disappear, leave this courtroom and find someplace where his foulness would be less noticeable.

"Madam," Mordecai said, pointing to a woman in the audience. A portly woman in a plain dress stared back in puzzlement. "Yes, madam, you in the dark blue dress and black hat.

"You know about the stink, don't you?"

The trial was the biggest show in Sanctuary, and the woman was flattered to have been chosen to play a part in it. Her exaggerated nod played to the townsfolk. Who in the world didn't know about the foul smell?

"I thought so," Mordecai said. "When Newcombe was talking about how bad this boy" — his finger settled on Judd huddled in the corner of the bench — "smells, you poked your neighbor with an elbow and held your nose."

Laughter rippled through the courtroom, and the woman held her nose again to emphasize the joke.

Driscoll stood.

"Your Honor, I don't see what this has to do with the case."

Mordecai answered the judge's inquiring look. "Your Honor, I am not an attorney.

I don't know all the subtleties of presenting my case, but I believe this is germane, and I would ask you to bear with me."

Harding, as much for curiosity as anything, nodded. "You may continue."

"The stink is terrible," Mordecai said. "It has permeated the very wood of this courtroom. It hangs in the air like a deep fog, confusing the senses. But dear lady, when you put your fingers over your nose, you weren't holding the stink out. You were holding it in."

A gasp squalled through the courtroom, but Mordecai cut it short.

"The stink doesn't come from Judd. It comes from all of you. It is the stink of hatred and ignorance untempered by compassion and reason. It is the stink of false pride and prejudice. That stink is an abomination on God's earth, and you people sit smugly in the reek of it, happy as pigs in a wallow.

"It is a strange place where a hate-filled man can drive a herd of cattle over a helpless victim and cannot be prosecuted because the victim is an Indian: a place where I sit charged because I had the audacity to feed the hungry among you, a people you are bludgeoning into oblivion by your ignorance and disregard."

The preacher sighed, hands on hips, in silence so deep everyone there heard the soft sound of breath leaving fifty sets of lungs.

"Most of you came here as refugees," he said, his voice soft again. "You were running from poverty and prejudice and hatred and lack of opportunity. And once you reached Sanctuary, you began victimizing other refugees you found here, others also seeking sanctuary from poverty and prejudice and hatred."

The preacher's eyes ranged over the crowd, still as a winter night. "Seek those people's forgiveness," he whispered, "if you ever hope to have God's."

The crowd sat in shocked silence. They seemed fascinated by their feet, studying them with a marked intensity, hiding their faces from Mordecai's eyes moving around the courtroom like a scythe.

And then the Reverend Eli was on his feet, face glowing dark red.

"Liar!" he shouted, his upraised arm swinging down like a club to crash across the room against Mordecai.

"Did I not tell you that this man is the great deceiver?" he shouted. "Did I not tell you that he would attempt to make you doubt the sanctity I have granted you? Did I not tell you that he would twist the scripture to fit his own evil ends?"

The roar of the Reverend's voice echoed through the courtroom, resounding against the walls, bouncing into the minds of the listeners.

"It is he, not you, who is evil. He consorts with drunkards and heathens. He would pull you down into the mire of sin and desolation. You are the soldiers of the Son of God."

And a roar went up from the crowd. The Reverend was right. They weren't the sinners. The preacher was on trial, not they. The preacher was a thief, not they. The stink came from the twelve-year-old boy hiding in his seat at the front of the courtroom, not from them.

They roared with righteous anger. The sound filled the room. It fed upon itself growing with each new voice as a fire grows with each branch thrown on it.

The sound was almost deafening, too loud to hear the rapping of Judge Harding's gavel, too loud for thought.

Sixteen

Jasper stood at Dirk Newcombe's elbow. He downed his whiskey in one gulp and held up the glass again for bartender Ben Johnson to fill.

Newcombe had been buying drinks for the house since leaving the courtroom, and Johnson had enough "dead soldiers" lined up below the bar to man a ghost brigade.

After the first order to keep the whiskey coming until he cut it off, Newcombe had been silent, glowering into the mirror in the back bar, Jasper doing all the talking for him. Jasper didn't mind a bit so long as the whiskey kept coming.

The crowd had turned surly with the alcohol and Jasper's prodding. When a fight broke out between two cowhands, blood lust rose in the throats of the crowd, men growling to the cadence of knuckles meeting bone. Newcombe let the fight go until one cowboy was beaten senseless.

And now Jasper was picking at the violence that underlined the room, focusing it on the man who had humiliated him that day at the slaughterhouse.

"Hell of a thing," the butcher said. "When a son-of-a-bitch like that comes into town calling himself a preacher and stirs the pot, causing problems for decent, law-abiding folk."

Arms saluted up and down the bar, glasses making one more trip to numbed lips.

"You really think there's a chance he might get off, Charley?"

Charley Benson had just come from the courthouse. He'd stayed to the end of the trial.

"Stranger things have happened," Benson said. "Talking to a shyster down in Glasgow one time, he told me that when the jury looks at the defendant when they're going out or coming in that's good news for him. When they don't, that's bad news.

"All those jurors were looking at the preacher. Some of them even smiling. All except for Elder Jackson. Course, that son-of-a-bitch never smiles — or looks you in the eye, for that matter."

A voice drifted in from farther down the bar. "He looked you in the eye that time you brought in the — uh — lady from Glasgow. He was right at the front of the Christian soldiers when they convinced her to move along to some more sinful place."

242

Laughter bounced against the back bar, and Benson stiffened. "Wasn't anything wrong with Gladys. She'd just had some tough times and — "

"SHUT UP!"

Newcombe's shout halted motion, brought absolute silence to the Silver Dollar. Arms were poised halfway to lips, conversations cut off as cleanly as with a scalpel. Not even the creak of chairs broke the silence as the uneasy men shifted their seats.

"When I first rode into this valley," Newcombe said, commanding everyone's attention, "the only justice a man had was what he could enforce himself. Well, I enforced the law — my law — on every damn Indian I saw. If they weren't stealing your cattle or murdering . . . your women, they were planning to.

"And I enforced the law on rustlers, every son-of-a-bitch I caught and everyone I suspected. I rode with Stuart's Stranglers and I was on that train with Granville, too. We made stops through Montana and clear into Dakota.

"More than sixty rustlers saw the light o' day when we rode up and never saw nothing but the doors to hell after that. We left 'em strung up to telegraph poles and cottonwood trees and whatever else was handy. Caught one man out on the prairie, nothing proper for hanging in sight. One of the cattlemen dropped a noose over his neck, dallied the end of a long rope around his saddle horn, and lit out at a gallop across the prairie. All that time the rustler was protesting his innocence, saying he was just riding through the country."

Newcombe's eyes burned through the crowd.

"Well, he protested until that horse came to the end of the rope. You could hear that man's neck break a hundred feet away, and he sailed through the air like his soul was trying to get a head start to hell. Damn near ruined Turk's saddle, and he still cusses about that today.

"Thing of it was that when there was no law in this country, there was more justice than there is now."

Jasper cut in. "Mr Newcombe's right. Hanging's the only thing fit for that son-of-bitch. Let's fit him for a rope right now."

A roar went through the bar, and the crowd turned mob surged toward the door with Jasper in the lead. No one heard Ben Johnson's protests, no one except Dirk Newcombe, who fixed the bartender with a look that left him flopping helplessly behind the bar like a fish on a hook.

* ★ *

The Reverend Eli stood on the courthouse steps, ringed by his Christian soldiers. The soldiers were his instrument, and he was playing them as an artist plays a violin.

At the beginning, his voice had been low, little more than a whisper. They had strained to hear him, edging closer to the top of the steps. And when he had their attention, when his voice held them mesmerized, he raised the volume a little at a time until the vowels and consonants and syllables bumped against their ears like the beat of ancient drums.

The Christian soldiers began swaying then, in time to the beat. Hallelujahs were popping out of the crowd like the first kernels in a pan of corn heating on a stove.

The Reverend was the heat in that stove, changing the character of the crowd, chasing away reason, pulling them in until they were raw nerves and sinews and bones and muscle serving the Reverend's will.

And then the mob from the Silver Dollar saloon rounded the corner of the courthouse, and the Reverend stood before his soldiers, telling them his prophecy had been proven true.

His voice thundered into their ears. "Have not the good people of Sanctuary come to join us in our battle against Satan?"

The resounding "YES!" pushed the Reverend back on the steps as though carried by a flood.

The Reverend Eli stood there, the sky darkening behind him and the wind rising, threatening to take his voice away.

"Then let us march, Christian soldiers. Let us battle the Evil One. Let us deliver earth of sin and stand shining in the face of the Lord."

The two mobs flowed together, one fueled with alcohol and the other with hate, both aimed like arrows at Mordecai's heart.

Judd sat uneasy at the table in the judge's chambers. The room was grand, walls finished in dark mahogany and lined with more books than Judd had ever seen. The table-desk was dark oak with heavy, curved legs and clawed feet.

Chairs, carved of the finest woods, were curved to fit the backs of men, but not twelve-year-olds. Judd sat straight-backed on the edge of his seat, out of place in the midst of such finery — and rancor.

Judge William Tecumseh Harding had stomped into the room, fuming still over the Reverend Eli's outburst and the Christian soldiers' exodus from the courtroom.

But the judge's curiosity about this strange man who seemed an odd mix of preacher, lawyer, and rustler poked through the judge's anger, and he had invited the defendant to join him for dinner in the judge's chamber — provided that no words were spoken about the case.

Mordecai would be pleased to join the judge under those circumstances, he said. Could a few of his friends join him? The judge had considered the preacher's request for a moment and decided that Mordecai's friends could corroborate his and Sheriff Timothy's statements that the case had not been discussed if the issue were raised.

But the judge sensed little danger there. Any objections would have to come from the prosecuting attorney, and County Attorney Thomas Driscoll seemed anxious to be shut of the case as soon as possible.

The judge sat down at the table, his eyes moving over Mordecai, Sheriff Timothy, Deputy Whimple, a woman Mordecai called Mary, one of Sanctuary's doctors, and the Indian boy Judd who had testified against the preacher.

An odd mix of friends, the judge thought.

He asked Mordecai to bless the food, and as the preacher spoke, the judge's rancor drained from him. He felt refreshed, eager to learn more about this strange man, this accused rustler. The two talked in hushed tones, broken by grins and chuckles.

Only after the meal was complete did Mordecai turn his attention to the others.

"Not long before you'll be leaving Sanctuary," he said to Mary, the question plain in his voice.

"No, not long." Mary's reply was tinged with regret. She had enjoyed her summer at the river rocks school, teaching the Indian children the mysteries of the white man's speech and paper scratching. She would miss "her children," Indian and white. And more.

The wilds of Montana had wrapped their web around her. She had been captivated by that first fall, cottonwoods transformed by the first frost to gold so pure and bright it seemed the sun had broken into shards and fallen to earth.

Winter came fierce as a warrior, challenging those it met to stand before its fury if they dared, or retreat.

In spring, the sun flirted with Montana like a young lover, showering the earth with a smile, only to skip away and then return, coquettish yet demanding. It was not until June, the month of the Sun Dance of most of the plains tribes, that the marriage was consummated and then Sanctuary languished with warmth and life.

The time Mary had spent in Sanctuary

had made her more aware, more sensitive to the world about her. In her walks along the river, she had felt at one with the land, as much a part of nature as the deer she occasionally frightened on the river bottom, her presence sending them crashing into a stand of willows or wild roses.

"No, not long," she repeated to Mordecai, her voice little more than a whisper.

"Don't rush off," the preacher said. "I've heard that the school board is having a hard time finding a replacement for you. Seems that word has spread about the little dance the Christian soldiers performed at the teacher-age. Not many want to be subjected to that."

The preacher's voice dropped. "I don't think anything like that will happen again.

"Since you'd be in a strong position for bargaining, you could likely insist that Judd and the others from the garden school be allowed to study with the other children."

Mary felt warmed by the preacher's beatific smile. At that moment, all her cares and worries and regrets seemed to be stripped away. She felt alive and full of hope and love.

"Yes, I could do that," she said. "There's no need to rush off."

"And Doc," the preacher asked, turning his attention to the old man. "Have you found where the wild crocus grows?"

Doc looked at the preacher, and when he spoke, his voice was little more than a whisper. "Yes, preacher, I've found where the wild crocus grows."

Mordecai smiled.

"You had better go, now. I'll talk to Judd a little later. Know that I will always love you."

"It sounds as though you're saying goodbye," Mary said.

Mordecai shook his head. "I'll always be with you. But you had better go now. Judd, you go, too. Take the extra plate to your grandmother."

"Go out the back, now, and no one will see you."

And the three stepped out of the room and down the hall, heels clicking across the polished hardwood, none of them wondering why it was important they were not seen.

Clouds were rising in the west and the sky was darkening. A storm seemed to be brewing, and the three leaned into the wind as they left the building. It seemed even then, even against the blasts of wind that popped in their ears, they could hear the rumble of thunder, still distant, but nearing.

Jasper and the Reverend Eli were side by side as they popped through the double doors at the front of the courthouse. The doors slammed against the walls, a hairline crack chasing across the glass in one. The doors tried to swing closed, only to be thrown once more against the wall by the crush of the mob.

The cracked pane crashed against the floor, shards skittering across the polished hardwood ahead of the mob, but the glass came to rest, momentum spent, and the mob moved on, carried by common purpose.

The door of the courtroom crashed open. Clerk of Court Melvin Jacobs was sitting at the evidence table, preferring solitude to the company of those less worthy than he. He looked up as the mob surged through the doors, eyes widening as he read intent on twisted faces. Jacobs tried to rise, only to step into Jasper's backhand as the big man reached the table.

A roar went up from the crowd as Jacobs tumbled back to crash against the railing. They left him there like an irrigation dam washed out by a flood, while they raged through the courtroom and up to the door of the judge's chambers.

The little knot of men there was more formidable than the clerk, and the mob slowed as though the flood had washed against a boulder in its path.

The boulder was Sheriff Timothy. Deputy

Whimple hovered behind, but his eyes were darting from the men to the back door. The mob was aching to kill, and Whimple knew it didn't matter much who.

A pistol appeared in Timothy's hand, the bore opening like the door to hell for those at the front of the mob, but they were being shoved toward the sheriff by the crush of those behind and couldn't stop.

Judge Harding was on his feet, eyes wild. "Get the hell out of my chambers, or I'll have you all in jail."

The judge didn't see Jasper's fist, swung low from his belt. He didn't feel it either, when it landed on his chin. The mob roared and surged forward another step.

Snick! The hammer clicked back on Timothy's pistol. When his voice came, it was even more menacing than the weapon he held in his hand.

"One step, and I'll go down shooting. Packed like you are, I figure I can take two of you at a shot as often as not.

"That means nine or ten of you will be in hell to welcome me. You're going to be first, Jasper. You'll get a slug all to yourself, right between your beady little eyes.

"Think, now! Nine or ten of you dying before I go down, and that's not counting how many Whimple takes before you step over him."

Whimple's eyes were wide, and he belatedly hauled his revolver out of his holster. He knew what the sheriff said was true. He knew too that the mob would kill them both if the sheriff squeezed his pistol's trigger.

Whimple swung the pistol as hard as he could, the barrel thumping behind the sheriff's ear. As Timothy sank to the floor, the mob surged forward. Whimple was shouting "Remember what I did when you vote for sheriff," but his voice was lost to the roar as the mob laid hands on Mordecai.

Outside, black clouds rolled in from the west, turning day to night. Lightning flashed through the clouds. Thunder rumbled, and the wind howled.

Judd huddled, hidden behind a lilac bush on the courthouse lawn, wishing he could help the preacher, afraid of what would happen if he tried.

The back door of the courthouse burst open, and the mob streamed through. Mordecai was at the front, hands bound behind his back, shoved along by the crowd. A wagon and horses waited at the door, and the preacher was thrown on the wagon bed, sprawling from the force of the fall.

For a moment, Judd couldn't see, the sting of tears stealing his vision. He wiped the tears from his eyes and saw that Mordecai had managed to push himself into a half-sitting position. Blood cut black lines from the preacher's mouth and nose in the dim light, and for a moment, he looked across the yard to the lilac bush.

Mordecai seemed to have smiled for a moment, but Judd couldn't be sure, his vision blurred by tears.

The wagon jolted across the courthouse lawn, dropped into the street, and turned east toward the cottonwoods lining the banks of the Milk River.

A steady roar rose from the crowd, the heat of their hatred driving away the chill from the storm winds from the west.

Judd crawled from the bush in growing darkness, jerking when a crack of lightning caught him mid-step.

He followed the wagon, darting from picket fence to shrub to the corners of backyard sheds, not noticing pale faces outlined in windows and staring after the mob.

The wagon had reached the edge of town, wheels jolting over clumps of sagebrush, Mordecai twisting to maintain his balance on the wagon bed.

Then Judd saw Jasper reach into the wagon — a whip! Jasper uncoiled it, and, with a flick of his wrist, sent the tip speeding toward

Mordecai's face. Mordecai tried to twist free, but his bound hands handicapped him.

Crack! The whip cut into Mordecai's face, and another trickle of blood coursed down his cheek. *Crack! Crack! Crack! Crack!* And above even the rattle of the wagon and the rumble of the storm came the sound of Jasper's laughter. Judd cringed, but he forced himself to run toward the sound, tears hiding the path from his feet.

A lone cottonwood, as big around at the base as a bar table, stood on the hill overlooking the river bottom. The wagon bounced to a stop below that tree and even in the darkness settling over the land, Judd could see the rope sailing over a limb pointing like an accusing finger toward the mountains to the west.

Two men climbed into the wagon box to jerk Mordecai to his feet. Mordecai stood, feet spread wide to balance himself, one man holding the preacher's arm while the other snatched like a kitten playing with a string at the rope dancing in the rising wind.

Then the noose began taking shape: first one loop, then another, the short end of the rope coiling around the loops to set the knot like fate. Too short! The hangman opened the loop, giving himself more working room, pulling the knot tight, but not too tight. He twisted the knot straight and stood there for a moment, admiring his work.

A roar rose from the mob, only to be lost in the scream of the wind. Judd found himself screaming, too, as he ran toward the wagon, ran toward this death in the making.

The two men climbed out of the wagon, and the Reverend Eli had his Bible out, and was shouting Revelations into the wind.

"And the great dragon was cast out, that old serpent called the Devil and Satan, which deceiveth the whole world: he was cast out into the earth, and his angels were cast out with him.

"And I heard a loud voice saying in heaven, Now is come salvation and strength, and the kingdom of our God, and the power of his Christ: for the accuser of our brethren is cast down, which accused them before our God day and night.

"And they overcame him by the blood of the Lamb, and by the word of their testimony; and they loved not their lives unto the death.

"Therefore rejoice, ye heavens, and ye that dwell in them. Woe to the inhabiters of the earth and of the sea! For the devil is come down unto you, having great wrath, because he knoweth that he hath but a short time."

Judd could feel the rage the Reverend was kindling in the mob, even before he reached the men farthest from the wagon. They stared, eyes glazed, and Judd sprinted past them, leaping before any arm could reach out to stop him.

He climbed to the seat of the wagon, swaying there from the wind and exhaustion.

"See me!" Judd pleaded. "Please see me, now. I am of the people, a heathen and a sinner, and of no worth.

"But, please hear me!

"Hear me. I will bark like a dog for you. I will catch raw meat in my mouth, if only you will hear me, now."

Judd shuffled into some dance steps on the wagon box. Sometimes dancing made him visible to the people of Sanctuary.

"The preacher is a good man. For a while, I thought that was not so. But I know it now. I know it deep in my soul. I have a soul. The preacher told me that. He told me, too, that God would listen to me if I spoke to him.

"If God will listen, can you not hear me once?

"If you must hang someone today, please hang me and let the preacher go.

"I will go gladly to the spirit world the preacher has told me about. I will not struggle. I will place the noose around my own neck.

"Hang me, please."

The boy's words shamed the mob, and it began to break up, the fringes carried away in the high wind like leaves in fall.

Judd, tears streaking his face, turned toward the preacher. Mordecai was smiling; his blood-streaked face seemed to glow in the growing darkness of the storm.

"You made them see you, Judd. Remember, I told you it is harder to be seen than to be invisible. They will never forget you now.

"Talk to Doc about practicing medicine. I think you will be a fine doctor. Pay attention to Mary. Her heart's big enough for the two of you. And listen to your grandmother. She knows more than she admits.

"You and Jack will have to keep the garden going, keep the people together. Tell them that I love them."

"Aren't you going to stay with us, then?" Judd asked, pleading.

A frown crossed the preacher's face like a shade. He shook his head, and at that moment the Reverend Eli's voice split the winds.

"Did I not tell you he is the great deceiver? Did I not tell you that he would play tricks on your minds to steal your souls?"

The Reverend's voice cracked through the howl of the wind and the rumble of distant thunder. The crowd had hearkened to the Reverend Eli too long to ignore him now. The trickle of men from the mob slowed and faces, stark white in the wind and the flash of lightning, turned one more time to face their accuser.

The Reverend's eyes were wide and wild, the wind tugged at his coat and sleeves and he seemed wraithlike, black-against-black.

"Gaze upon me," the Reverend screamed into the wind. "Know that you are looking upon the face of the son of God. I am Jesus Christ come to deliver the world of sin."

The townspeople stood transfixed in horror. In the wind and the darkness and the flashes of lightning, they saw the Reverend Eli Timpkins — and themselves — clearly for the first time. They were terrified by that vision.

The mob shattered, carried away by the wind and the realization of what they had almost done. One man broke from the others and stepped toward the wagon, his knife blade gleaming as he held it up to Judd to cut the noose from Mordecai's neck.

"No!" the Reverend shouted.

Eli grabbed the whip from Jasper's hands and sent the tip curling toward the nearest horse. The crack of the whip against the horse's side was lost in the *Crack* of a bolt of lightning that flashed bright as the sun.

Judd was thrown to the bed of the wagon as the horses bolted. He looked back to see Mordecai swinging in the wind. The rain came then, drops stinging as they fell, mixing with his tears and blotting out his vision.

THORNDIKE PRESS hopes you have enjoyed this Large Print book. All our Large Print titles are designed for easy reading, and all our books are made to last. Other Thorndike Large Print books are available at your library, through selected bookstores, or directly from the publisher. For more information about current and upcoming titles, please call or mail your name and address to:

THORNDIKE PRESS
PO Box 159
Thorndike, Maine 04986
800/223-6121
207/948-2962